P9-ARE-265

The First Run of the Pony Express:

DEADLY DETOUR...

"Ain't you boys a mite old to be playing Injun?" Morgan Bunker couldn't help feeling somewhat proud of himself as he trained his gun on his would-be ambushers—two white men dressed like Paiute Indians.

The men glared at him, saying nothing.

"If you figure on foolin' anybody, you ought to study up on the ways of Injuns. For one thing, they mount from the right side of the horse, not the left, the way one of you boys did up there on the hill."

Damn, Morgan thought to himself. This was really going to slow the mail down. Even though he'd known the many probable hazards before he started, Morgan had hoped that this first run of the new Pony Express Company would go without a hitch.

"Now you just unbuckle those gunbelts," the young express rider said, "and toss them down easy."

One of the men made a sudden grab for his pistol, and Morgan fired. The slug caught the man high on the inside of the leg and he dropped the gun and fell to his knees.

As Morgan swung the barrel of his Colt over to cover the other man, he felt a searing pain in his left side, and heard the crack of a rifle ringing in his ears . . .

The Making of America Series

THE EXPRESS RIDERS

Lee Davis Willoughby

A DELL/JAMES A. BRYANS BOOK

Published by
Dell Publishing Co., Inc.
1 Dag Hammarskjold Plaza
New York, New York 10017

Copyright © 1982 by Garrison, Inc.

All rights reserved. No part of this book
may be reproduced or transmitted in any form
or by any means, electronic or mechanical, including
photocopying, recording or by any information storage
and retrieval system without the written permission
of the Publisher, except where permitted by law.

Dell ® TM 681510, Dell Publishing Co., Inc.

ISBN: 0-440-02249-5

Printed in the United States of America

First printing—September 1982

1

In early March of 1860 the main street of St. Joseph, Missouri was shinbone-deep in gluey mud from the melting of the winter snows. The mood of the town, however, was buoyant. For once they had stolen a prize from their larger neighbor to the south, Kansas City. Russell, Majors and Waddell, operators of a huge freight wagon system, had chosen St. Joe as the eastern jump-off point for their exciting new venture, the Pony Express.

In the headquarters of the Central Overland Express half a hundred young men sat nervously waiting to be sworn in as riders. Across the street in the Singletree Saloon at least as many celebrated. The air in the Singletree was steamy from the massed bodies and fouled with the smoke of cheap cheroots, but the mood was jubilant. The men drank and laughed and hollered at each other, congratulating themselves and their town on being a part of history.

One customer in the Singletree who did not join in the general hooraw was Cherokee Joe Bunker. He stood weaving at the bar with his hand wrapped around a whiskey glass, scowling down at the wet circles left on the dark wood by previous glasses. He spat carelessly in the direction of the cuspidor at his feet and took another swallow of the whiskey. It was rotgut, but in the end it got you the same place as expensive bourbon.

A stranger edged into the space at the bar next to Joe. A cowhand at one of the nearby spreads, from the look of his outfit.

"Big day for the town, ain't it?" the stranger said.

Joe continued to stare down at the bar as though he hadn't heard.

"Care to join me in a drink to celebrate?"

This time Joe turned deliberately away from the other man.

"I'm talkin' to you, mister," the cowboy said.

Cherokee Joe set his whiskey glass down carefully and turned back to face him. His pale eyes stared unblinkingly into those of the cowboy. It was the same pale glare that had paralyzed stage drivers into throwing down the money box with no backtalk in his days as a road agent.

"I don't feel like celebratin'," Joe said in a low, dangerous voice. "And if I did, it wouldn't be with you."

The cowboy's gaze fell away. "Just tryin' to be sociable," he muttered, and moved away to find another spot to do his drinking.

Joe touched a match flame to one of the evil-smelling stogies the management handed out and returned his glowering attention to the bar in front of him.

There was a murmur of surprise from the direction of the entrance, then all talk and laughter in the saloon ceased abruptly. Heads turned and men craned their necks to look toward the batwing doors. Standing there, holding the two doors apart, was a woman. A tall, red-haired, long-legged, fine-chested woman. She stood there for a minute, her gaze ranging over the faces of the men inside. Her eyes flashed green and angry, and finally settled on the swaying back of Cherokee Joe Bunker.

The woman let the doors flap shut behind her and marched across the gritty floor of the big room while the dumbfounded men made way for her. She pushed her way in to the bar next to Joe and stood there with her fists planted on her well-rounded hips.

"I might have known I'd find you in here pickling your liver," she said.

The bartender shook himself into action and hurried over to where they stood. "I'm sorry, ma'am, but ladies aren't allowed in here."

She turned the blazing green eyes on the bartender. "In the first place, I'm already in, and in the second, who says I'm a lady?"

While the bartender stood with his mouth flapping, the red-haired woman turned back to Cherokee Joe. "Do you know where your boys are right now?"

"You mean Morgan and Jack?"

"That's who I mean unless you been holding out on me and got more than two sons."

"Morgan's across the street in the Central Overland office gettin' hisself signed up to ride for that blamed Pony Express."

"I know all about that," the red-haired woman said. "It's Jack that I'm mainly concerned with since he's supposed to be working for me."

Joe looked puzzled. "Ain't he down to Kansas City with your outfit?"

"No he ain't," the woman said emphatically.

Joe Bunker scratched his head and tried to digest this piece of information. Meanwhile, the rest of the men in the Singletree stood with their drinks forgotten, cigars smouldering between their teeth, chaws tucked away in one cheek, while they stared at the unaccustomed sight of a well-dressed woman in a saloon. And right up at the bar, no less. Down in Kansas City, where they were used to Jessie McKee and her ways, the men were no longer shocked when she barged into their bailiwick. When her husband died five years before Jessie took over the Ace Freighters and ran the company more ruthlessly than any man. She also made a lot more money than the late Sam McKee ever had, and that gave her certain privileges that women were not usually accorded. However, up here in St. Joseph, at the edge of the western frontier, the only women seen in a saloon were the whores that came in with the railroad. This redhead, the men in the Singletree soon saw, bore herself much too proud to be any kind of a whore.

Cherokee Joe went through the business of relighting his cold stogie while he recovered from the surprise of Jessie's sudden appearance.

"Well," he said, "if Jack ain't down there with your outfit, maybe you can tell me where he is?"

"He's across the street with his brother fixin' to sign up with those vultures Russell, Majors and Waddell, that's where."

"He can't do that, he works for you."

"Why don't you just march over there and remind him of that?"

Cherokee Joe scowled around at the men who were watching them attentively. "Reckon I'll do just that," he said. With a belated show of male authority he pushed past Jessie and shouldered his way to the door. The widow McKee followed, ignoring the muttered remarks of the men as she passed.

Out in front of the saloon she stood on the board-walk in front of the saloon and watched Joe slog through the mud toward the offices of the Central Overland. For a moment her stern expression relaxed into something like tenderness. But only for a moment.

2

In the wooden building across from the Singletree Saloon that housed the headquarters of the Central Overland Express Co., the desks of all the clerks and order-takers had been pushed over against one wall. In their place were rows of wooden benches now occupied by fifty eager young men. These had passed preliminary interviews and been weeded out of of several hundred candidates for jobs as riders on the Pony Express.

The average age of the men was twenty or even younger, and they were on the small side. To meet the tough cross-country schedules set by Mr. Russell and his partners, a horse, even a superior animal, should not be asked to carry a man weighing much more than 140 pounds.

Near the back of the room 18-year-old Morgan Bunker sat beside his brother. Morgan, at 5′ 10″, was taller than most of the applicants, but he was lean and wiry, with powerful forearms. His horsemanship was well known to the company, as he had worked as an outrider for their freight wagons for eighteen months.

Morgan's brother Jack, a year younger, was shorter and heavier through the body. His shaggy black hair and heavy eyebrows favored their father, while Morgan was sandy-haired and lighter complexioned, like their mother had been.

At the far end of the big room, on a platform with a lectern in front of him, stood a broad-shouldered man of about forty. He had a tough, weathered face, and looked uncomfortable in his city clothes. This was Bolivar Roberts, who was in charge of finding the best horses and men available for this new venture of his employers. He looked out over the rows of young men and spoke in a gravelly voice that snapped with authority.

"In just about three and a half weeks," Roberts said, "the first man is going to ride out of here carrying the U.S. mail for the Pony Express. The Central Overland Express plans on hiring 125 riders here and out in California to get the show started. I'll be picking out the first batch today from among you men."

He paused and looked around. "To get as far as this room all of you had to show something in the way of guts and good sense. Whether you're finally chosen or not, you can walk out of here with your heads up. Now I've got a few things to say to the lot of you about this operation, then I'm going to talk to each of you, one at a time. By sundown we'll know which of you will sign on as riders for the Pony Express."

Jack Bunker leaned over close to his older brother and whispered, "Why do we have to listen to all this chin waggin'?"

Morgan gave him a sharp look. "You just hush and listen to Mr. Roberts. Won't hurt you a bit, and you might learn something."

"Back in January," Roberts continued, "Mr. William

Russell gave his personal word to President Buchanan that on April 3 we would begin a mail run between St. Joe and Sacramento, California that will be faster than anything ever tried before. That gave us just 65 days to get equipped and ready to go. We've used up more than half of the time, and I don't mind telling you it's been one whale of a job. We worked on the most important part first." He paused with a twinkle in his eye before going on. "No, that part wasn't you boys, it was the horses."

The young men in the room chuckled and shifted to more relaxed positions on the benches.

"We went out and bought the best horseflesh we could find. We paid one hundred fifty up to two hundred dollars apiece for them, and I don't have to tell you men that'll buy a lot of animal. Our ponies have to be fast— fast and strong because they're going to have to run non-stop between our relay stations, some 20 miles, at better than 12 miles an hour."

The young men on the benches murmured appreciatively and exchanged looks.

"But it's not only the horses that have to be the best," Bolivar Roberts went on. "You men are all hand-picked too. You've got to be the best too. That's why we're starting our riders out at one hundred dollars a month, plus room and board. Do your job, and you can go up to one hundred twenty dollars. For some of the toughest runs the company will go to one hundred fifty."

Somebody out in front whistled at the figures.

"That's right," Roberts said, "there aren't many places a young fella can earn that kind of money. But let me tell you here and now, you will earn it. You will travel fast over some of the roughest, most God-forsaken country you ever saw. You'll freeze in the mountains and you'll fry on the desert. You'll spend some hungry days and nights, and you'll cross miles and miles of alkali dust with not a drop of water. Your run will be 55 miles in the mountains and 120 miles on the prairies, and you'll do it with only your pony for company. At the end of your run you'll be dog-tired, but if for some reason the next man can't carry on, you'll climb back in the saddle and take his run too."

Roberts stopped talking for a minute. The only sound in the room was the occasional scrape of a boot on the bare floor.

"I wouldn't blame any man here if he excused himself right now and ambled out." Roberts paused for a long moment, then continued. "Well, I didn't think any of you would, but I wanted to give you the opportunity. Now I know all you men can ride, or you wouldn't be here. I know you're tough and you're smart, but that's not all it takes to ride for the Pony Express. It takes character."

At that moment the door at the front of the building burst open and Cherokee Joe Bunker stood in the doorway. He was steady now, having fought off the effects of the liquor on his way across the street.

"We're having a private meeting in here, mister," Roberts said.

Bunker spat tobacco juice on the floor. "Piss on your meeting. I come to talk to my boys."

Roberts stepped out from behind the lectern. "I don't like that kind of talk, mister." The room went deadly quiet. Roberts undid the button of his frock coat casual-like, giving them all a look at the revolver on his hip.

Cherokee Joe, not a man to back off, glared at him from the doorway. By the terms of his release from territorial prison he was not supposed to carry firearms, but such rules didn't carry much muscle outside the big cities. From where Morgan and Jack sat, they could see that their father was wearing a heavy old Walker Colt. At a clumsy four and a half pounds, it was no weapon for a fast draw contest, but it could throw a .44-caliber slug way out there and put a pretty good hole in a man.

Quickly the Bunker boys were on their feet. They hustled back to flank Cherokee Joe, each grabbing an arm.

"He's our father, Mr. Roberts," said Morgan. "We'll take care of him."

Bolivar Roberts gave them a cool nod and stepped back behind the lectern, buttoning his coat. A collective sigh went up from the young men seated on the benches. It might have been either relief or disappointment.

Between them the two boys wrestled Cherokee Joe outside. Morgan reached back and pulled the door closed behind them.

"Let go of me, Goddamn it," Bunker yelled. "I'll take on the both of you right here and now, and don't you think I can't do it."

The boys let go of their father and stepped back, watching him warily.

"What kind of sons are you, anyway?" Joe demanded. "Wouldn't even stick up for your own father. Did you hear the way that old galoot talked to me?"

"Bolivar Roberts ain't no older'n you are, Pa," Morgan said. "And you did bust into his meeting without being invited."

Joe Bunker looked all around with a scowl, as though trying to find something he could get good and mad at. He settled on his younger son.

"What in the hell are you doin' in there, anyway,

Jack? You already got yourself a job with Ace Freighters."

"Jack ain't under bond to the Widow McKee," Morgan said.

"Now just what do you mean by that?" Joe growled.

"Nothin', Pa, only that Jack's old enough to choose his own path."

Joe faced his younger son. "Why don't you speak up for yourself, boy?"

Jack shuffled his boots uncomfortably over the wood plank sidewalk. "Central Overland's payin' a hundred dollars a month to start, Pa, and Morgan says they're a straight outfit to work for."

"Are you sayin' Jessie McKee ain't runnin' a straight outfit?"

"No, 'course not," Jack said quickly. "It's just that Morgan here said there was a chance for me to get on with the Pony, and—"

"You lettin' your brother lead you around by the ear now?"

"I just told him about Mr. Russell's idea for carryin' the mail a new way," Morgan said.

"Old Man Russell ain't got the mail contract sewed up yet," Joe said. "Jessie McKee figures Ace Freighters can do a better job followin' the Butterfield route down south out of Kansas City."

"The Butterfield route's too long," Morgan said. "And there's six hundred miles of desert between El Paso and Fort Yuma that they gotta use mules on now. No lone horse and rider could make it."

"I didn't come here to argue with you," said Cherokee Joe. "You already work for this outfit, so you can do as you please. But you, Jack, are you gonna let your brother tell you what to do, or are you gonna start bein' your own man?"

Jack looked unhappily from his father to his brother. "I reckon I do owe the Widow McKee somethin'."

Joe threw an arm around his younger son's shoulder. "That's the way to talk, boy." He glanced across the street. "Most likely the widow's back at the hotel now. Let's go on over and tell her she's got at least one rider she can count on."

The two brothers faced each other. "What Pa says is true," Jack said. "Russell and the rest ain't got no signed contract to carry the mail yet."

"We'll get one, soon as we show them people in Washington what we can do," Morgan said.

"Maybe. But I reckon I do have an obligation to Ace Freighters."

"Whatever you say," Morgan told him. "I gotta go now."

He turned and walked back into the office of the Central Overland. His father and brother headed back across the muddy street.

3

CHEROKEE Joe and Jack Bunker clumped down the boardwalk to the entrance to the Regal Hotel. Before going in they used the metal scraper as best they could to gouge the mud from their boots. Still, the clerk behind the desk gave them the fisheye when they walked through the carpeted lobby. Joe glared back at the man and he quickly got busy with something else.

Father and son climbed to the second floor where Jessie McKee had taken one of the Regal's best rooms overlooking the street. Joe knocked on the door and it was opened almost immediately by the widow herself.

" 'Lo, Jessie. I brung the boy."

"I can see that," the red-haired woman said impatiently. "Bring him on in and try not to leave too much of that Missouri mud on the furniture."

Joe and his son entered the room gingerly. It had a huge canopy bed and a smaller bed partially concealed by a folding Chinese screen. The room had a coal-burning stove of its own and a carved mahogany commode for the wash basin. The curtains on the windows were real lace and the wallpaper had an intricate

17

pattern of vines and little roses. Joe figured the room must have set the widow back a good five dollars a night.

Over by the Chinese screen a blonde girl of about sixteen stood watching the men curiously. She had enormous blue eyes and an Eastern-cut taffeta dress of the same color. Her figure was already that of a woman.

Jessie's voice softened when she spoke to the girl. "Beth, you run along now and pick out the goods for your new dress."

"Yes, Mama." The girl's voice was throaty, with an appealing hoarseness. Young Jack Bunker could not take his eyes off her.

"It's likely I won't be here when you get back," Jessie continued, "so lock yourself in the room and wait for me."

"Yes, Mama."

Jessie glanced over at the Bunkers. "And don't open the door for anybody but me."

"No, Mama." The girl bobbed her head at the two men and went out.

"Mighty pretty gal," said Cherokee Joe. "She must be the daughter you been keepin' at that fancy school back east."

"Yes, she's my daughter," Jessie admitted.

"Got a complexion that favors you, Jessie. Smooth as cream."

"Never mind about my daughter. We got business to talk."

"Sure thing," said Joe amiably.

Jack Bunker continued to stare at the door where Beth had gone out. It took a sharp nudge from his father to regain the boy's attention.

Jessie sat down in a chair at a small writing table

over by the window. She had taken off the hat she wore for her foray into the saloon, and her hair was pulled back severely the way she did it when she wanted to look like a business woman. Before she started to speak there was a sharp rap at the door.

"Yes?"

The door opened and a narrow-shouldered man with a weak moustache looked into the room. There was an inch-long knife scar that pulled up one corner of his mouth to expose a couple of yellow teeth.

"Not now, Smiler," Jessie said. "Come back in a few minutes."

The man shot a cold look at the Bunkers and withdrew, closing the door behind him.

"Who's that snake?" Joe asked.

"He's one of my men," Jessie said, "and a damn good one." She turned her attention to the younger Bunker. "Well, Jack, does this mean you're back with us?"

Jack shifted uncomfortably under the steady green gaze. "Reckon I am, ma'am."

"Onliest reason he was over there was to find out what them Russell people was up to," said Joe.

"I'm glad to hear that." Jessie gave the young man a smile that showed even white teeth. "I'd hate to think I was losing a fine, strong young fella like you to my business rivals."

"No chance of that," Joe assured her. "Jack here is true blue to Ace Freighters. Ain't that a fact, boy?"

"Yes'm, that's the way of it," Jack agreed.

"Good," Jessie said. "I've got plans for you in my company, Jack. But we can talk about that later." She picked her bag up from the floor and dug through it for a change purse. She snapped it open and poked at the coins inside. "We'll start off by giving you a raise in pay. Here's ten dollars advance. I understand there's a couple of places in St. Joe where a young man can have a pretty good time on that."

"Yes'm, I reckon there is." Jack accepted the offered money and stood uncertainly for a moment. At a signal from his father he nodded to the widow and left the room.

Cherokee Joe strolled across the room to the writing table where Jessie sat. She stood up to meet him. Joe wrapped an arm around her. He dropped one hand to give a squeeze to her firm rump.

"Talkin' about fun," he said, "how about you and me gettin' some use out of that nice big bed?"

Jessie wrinkled her nose at him. "When was the last time you had a bath?"

"Hell, I don't know. Two weeks, maybe three. I been on the trail. What difference does it make?"

"You smell like a goat."

"You didn't complain none about the way I smelled last Saturday at your place in K.C."

"We had all the windows open that night." Jessie moved out of his grasp. She took another coin from her purse and held it out to him. "Get yourself a bath and a shave and come back tonight."

"What about the girl?"

"She'll stay here. I've arranged for another room where I can conduct my . . . business."

Joe frowned at the coin she still held out to him. "I don't like takin' money from no woman."

"Go ahead." Jessie softened her tone. "Tonight you can pay me back good and proper."

Joe palmed the coin with a show of reluctance. "This don't mean you're gonna expect me to take a bath ever' time we hit the mattress now, I hope."

"That would be asking too much," Jessie agreed.

"On your way out tell Smiler to come back in, will you?"

Joe gave her a solid pat on the ass to remind her who was the man here, then he went out into the hall. The man with the scarred lip was standing across from the room using a double-edged Arkansas toothpick to pare his fingernails.

"She wants you in there now," Joe said, giving the other man a long once-over.

Smiler looked back at him with a little twitch of that queer crooked mouth. He said nothing, but opened the door to Jessie's room and walked in. Joe wondered if this was his competition for the widow. If so, he and Smiler were going to have to face off one day. Cherokee Joe was right possessive about what he figured was his.

Jessie was back sitting at the writing table when Smiler came in. "What do you see in that draggle-tail old bandit, anyhow?" he asked.

Jessie's eyes flashed. "That's none of your damn business. And if you got any doubts about how much of a man Joe Bunker is, you'll stay a lot healthier keeping them to yourself."

"Sure, Jessie. I didn't mean nothin'."

The red-haired woman glared at him for a moment longer, then relaxed. "All right, forget it. I want to hear about Russell's plan for the Pony Express. Do you think he can pull it off? You've been over the route; can his riders cover the two thousand miles between here and Sacramento in ten days?"

Smiler pulled a folded map out of his jacket pocket and spread it on the table. It showed the western half of the country with a squiggly black line drawn in ink between St. Joseph and Sacramento.

"If everything goes right for 'em, they can make it," Smiler said.

"What about Indians?"

"The Kickapoos are friendly. The Shoshones and the Pawnees ain't likely to cause 'em any trouble neither. The Cheyennes, though, and the Paiutes, they could be another story. 'Specially the Paiutes. Word is they're spoilin' for a fight."

"Good for them. The trouble is, we can't be sure the Paiutes will do anything to this one rider."

"Can't be sure of nothin' with Injuns."

Jessie studied the map with her lips pressed together. "Are they likely to run into trouble with the weather?"

"Can't count on it. There's prob'ly a lot of snow left in the high country through the Sierra Nevadas, but it'll be melting a month from now when the Pony rider's due to go through."

Jessie traced a finger along the black line drawn on the map. "What are these heavy black dots?"

"Them's the home stations where the riders'll start and finish up their runs. They're puttin' in 120 of them, more or less. In between them's the relay stations with the fresh horses."

"Can the Central Overland get all this operating in time?"

"They're sure as hell workin' at it. They been buyin' horses from here to Kentucky. Out in California too. Payin' top dollar. They got a good start hirin' riders and station keepers. And I hear they're busy buildin' the stations wherever there ain't already a stage depot they can use."

"It sounds like that old buzzard Russell and his partners have sunk a pile of money into this."

"They're out to win the contract, that's for sure."

"We've got to see that they don't get it, Smiler." Jessie gazed at him levelly.

He poked at his exposed teeth with a thumbnail and waited for her to go on.

"Russell, Majors and Waddell aren't the only ones with a lot invested here. I spread a good deal of money among certain people in Washington to make sure they're in no hurry about awarding the mail contract. If the Pony Express screws up its first run across country, our case will be a whole lot stronger."

"You're sayin' maybe we should help 'em screw up, is that it?"

"That's it, except there's no maybe about it."

The man scratched his bony jaw. "Just how far are you willin' to go to see that the Pony Express don't ride in safe with that first load of mail?"

"Just as far as we have to, Smiler."

"Lots of accidents could happen to a lone rider over all that territory."

"I wouldn't be surprised."

"There's spots where one false step would put horse and rider over a cliff."

Jessie watched him, saying nothing.

"Or even simpler, one of their riders might get shot out of the saddle." He looked quickly at Jessie for a reaction. She did not flinch.

"It'd prob'ly be blamed on Injuns," Smiler said.

"I don't care who gets blamed, as long as it isn't Ace Freighters."

Smiler leaned down to point at the map. "One good spot for trouble is—"

"I don't want to hear about it, Smiler, I just want it to happen. I plan to be in Sacramento on February 13, and I don't want to see any rider from the Central Overland coming in straight up."

"Leave it to me," Smiler said.

"You'd better get the men you need together and start riding."

Smiler folded up the map and stuck it back in his pocket. He crossed the room to the door, where he turned back just before going out.

"See you in Sacramento," he said.

4

Bolivar Roberts spent the afternoon interviewing the young men who wanted to become riders for the Pony Express. He took them one by one into a small office off to one side of the big room, sat them down across the desk, and talked to them. From his observations and a few questions he had to decide whether they were made of the right stuff.

Looking into the eager, nervous young faces Roberts saw himself twenty years ago. He wished heartily that he could be on the other side of the desk now, just starting out on this great new adventure. Impatiently he yanked himself back from such woolgathering and studied the applicant who had just come in and taken the other chair. He wore a floppy wool hat and kept his head down.

"What's your name, fella?"

"Canliss, Mr. Roberts." The man did not raise his head.

"How old are you, Canliss?"

The man cleared his throat. "Twenty-five."

"That so? Take off your hat."

Canliss looked up, surprised. "Huh?"

"Take off your hat, please."

Reluctantly the man pulled off the wool hat and sat twisting it nervously in his hands. His hair was wispy and had streaks of gray in it.

"You're no more twenty-five than I am," Roberts said, not unkindly.

"I'm only thirty-one, and that's the God's truth," Canliss said earnestly. "I'm strong and healthy as an ox, and I can ride with any of them young bucks out there."

"I don't doubt that you can," Bolivar Roberts said, "but riding for the Pony Express is young man's work. Even twenty-five is pushing the limit."

Canliss looked as though he had been punched in the stomach.

"Stick around, though. There might be a job for you at one of the stations if you're good with horses."

"Thanks, Mr. Roberts." The old man of thirty-one pulled on his hat and walked out of the office. Bolivar Roberts looked after him, shaking his head sadly.

The next few men he checked out were young enough and strong enough, and he signed most of them up. One he turned down because of a suspicious cough, another who showed signs of old frostbite on his hands. Pony riders would have to be able to handle any part of the route through prairie, desert, or mountains between here and Sacramento. There could be no question about their physical shape.

As he neared the bottom of the list Roberts called in a candidate named Laidlaw. The young man leaned back in the chair and grinned confidently at the superintendent.

"What kind of experience you got?" Roberts asked.

"Been a wrangler since I was big enough to sit a horse."

"Where was your last job?"

"The Lazy L spread out of Tulsa."

"Pretty good rider, are you?"

"I can ride anything with four legs."

"Not drunk, you can't."

Laidlaw's eyes widened innocently. "What're you talkin' about?"

"Something in your coat pocket clunked against the chair when you sat down. Sounded like a bottle."

The young man gave Roberts a man-to-man grin. He pulled a pint bottle of rye whiskey out of his jacket. "Just a little snake bite remedy."

"Think you're going to meet up with a rattler in here? I could smell the booze on you the minute you walked in the door."

"Aw, a man's got to have a little snort now and again just to keep the red in his blood." He looked back over his shoulder, then grinned at Roberts and held out the pint. "Maybe you could use a little swig yourself."

Roberts' eyes hardened. "When you work for Russell, Majors and Waddell you don't drink intoxicating liquor."

Laidlaw stared at him. "What the hell kind of a rule is that?"

"You also do not use profane language. You can get out of here now."

The young wrangler, no longer confident, shoved the pint bottle back into his coat and stumbled to his feet. "Sounds to me like you got a bunch of sissies workin' for this outfit."

"I'll be glad to meet you after my working day is through and discuss that," Roberts said.

Young Laidlaw took a quick look at Roberts' face and hurried out of the office without having any more to say.

Roberts talked to the last few men who remained on the list and passed them all. He stood up and stretched. It had been a full day. He walked to the door and beckoned to Morgan Bunker. The young man got up from the bench and followed him into the small office.

"Sit down, Morgan," Roberts said. "I hope you don't mind my leaving you for last."

"I'm not in a hurry to go anyplace," Morgan said.

"There's no need for me to ask you any questions. I know your work with the Central Overland, and there's no doubt you'll make a fine rider for the Pony Express."

"I'll do my best."

"I know you will. In fact, I think so highly of you that I wanted you to ride the first leg of the first run out of St. Joe come April 3."

Morgan brightened. "That'd surely be an honor, Mr. Roberts."

The older man held up a hand. "Hold on. I said I wanted you to, but I ain't running this outfit. Mr. Russell had another idea, and he's the boss."

Morgan could not suppress a look of disappointment.

"Mr. Russell has a boy named Billy Richardson in mind to ride the first leg."

"I know him," Morgan said. "He's good."

"Sure, he's good. You're all good. But I still got something special in mind for you."

"That so?"

"As an outrider for our freight wagons you've had occasion more than once to come up against Indians, if I'm not mistaken."

"I have met up with a few," Morgan admitted.

"How do you feel about them?"

"Feel?"

"There's some people like to say the only good Indian is a dead Indian."

"That's hogwash," Morgan said. "Their ways sometimes look peculiar to us, but I reckon ours do to them too. Injuns are people, some good, some bad, same as white men. They was here first, so I figure you can't blame them too much for gettin' upset when we move into their huntin' grounds."

"I agree. Can you talk to them?"

"Not in their own language. Shoot, they got more different lingos than a dog got fleas. Even the same tribe don't all talk the same."

"I know that," Roberts said, "but you can sign with them, can't you?"

"Enough to get by. The plains Injuns all use pretty much the same signs."

"Good. I want you to ride the leg between Three Fools Creek and Carson City."

"That's Paiute country," Morgan said.

"That's right, and about as dangerous a stretch of ground as there is on the whole run. I need a man riding it who I've got confidence in. Any reason why you wouldn't want it?"

"I'll be proud to ride it, Mr. Roberts."

"I'll shake your hand on that," Roberts said.

Both men stood up and exchanged a grip.

"I'm sorry it didn't work out with your brother," Roberts said.

"Couldn't be helped," Morgan said. "I reckon Jack's still got some growin' up to do."

"I reckon." The superintendent took out his heavy gold watch and thumbed open the cover. "I advise you to get yourself a good night's sleep tonight. There'll be a special stage leaving at dawn tomorrow heading west."

"I'll be ready," Morgan said. He walked out of the Central Overland office feeling like he'd just been elected governor.

5

I⊤ was late afternoon when Morgan came out of the Central Overland office. There was a bite in the air. He pulled the sheepskin collar of his coat up around his chin and grinned to himself. He was an honest-to-God Pony Express rider, assigned personally by Bolivar Roberts to one of the toughest legs of the cross-country run. He felt like celebrating, but he knew Mr. Roberts was right—he would need a good night's sleep with the long stagecoach ride commencing early tomorrow morning. He quickened his step toward the east end of town where he was staying with his father and brother in a dollar-a-night room at the New Continental Hotel and Cafe.

Morgan's one regret was that Jack hadn't stuck it out with him. He didn't trust that Ace Freighters outfit. How could a man trust anything that was run by a woman anyhow? With Jack and him both working for the Pony, they could have had some good times together, really got to know each other as men.

But Morgan was not about to let Jack's decision dampen his good mood. He breathed deeply of the cool, clean air and marched proud down the wooden sidewalk.

Morgan slowed his step as he approached a dry goods store down near the end of the street. There seemed to be some kind of commotion out in front.

As he got closer Morgan saw there was a pretty blonde girl standing at the edge of the walk looking helplessly across the muddy street toward a horse and buggy on the other side. An unshaven young cowboy stood over there holding the horse. Out in the middle of the street two of his scruffy friends stood knee-deep in mud, laughing nasty-like and beckoning the girl to come on. Behind the girl the old storekeeper and his wife stood flapping their hands ineffectually at the liquored-up cowboys.

Morgan came to a stop a little ways away. Nobody paid any attention to him.

"You can just bring my horse and rig right back over here," the girl demanded in a voice as firm as she could muster.

One of the cowboys in the street gave her a gap-toothed grin. "Well, now, I don't know if we can do that without a little somethin' in return. Tell you what, you give each of us a little kiss and we'll give you a ride up on our shoulders over to your buggy." He turned to his pal beside him and to the one holding the horse. "How about that, fellers, don't that sound fair?"

The other two snickered and nodded their heads.

"There, you see," said the talkative one, "just one little kiss for me and my friends and we'll tote you across the street high and dry." He looked around at his pals and they all snickered some more.

"I'll do no such a thing!" the girl said.

"Well, now, you'd best think again, unless you want to get them petticoats all muddied up."

Morgan walked up and stood beside the girl. He gave the gap-toothed cowboy a hard look. "I think you fellers ought to do like the lady says and bring her rig on back over here."

The cowboys stared at him, then looked to the one who had been doing all the talking.

"How do you figure this is any business of yours?" he said.

"It ain't. I'm just passin' along some advice."

"I don't recollect askin' for any, so you might as well be on your way."

"Gladly," Morgan said. "Just as soon as you bring back the lady's horse and buggy."

"Are you fixin' to make me do it?"

"If need be."

The cowboy unbuckled his gunbelt and passed it over to his companion. He was a little drunk, but not enough to get involved in gunplay. Especially not here in St. Joe, where the law was strong and the frivolous shooting of citizens was not looked on kindly.

Morgan was unarmed, having left his guns in the care of the desk clerk at the New Continental. He saw no need to pack irons into town for a business meeting. He sized up the cowboy waiting for him down in the street. The man had a good twenty pounds on him, but there was a look of flabbiness where he should have been hard. Out of the corner of his eye Morgan could also see the blonde girl. She was standing beside him looking at him with the biggest blue eyes he had seen in his life. He knew right then that he was going to whip this cowboy.

The man in the street waved his friends back out of the way, then turned back to face Morgan.

"Any time you're ready, Pilgrim."

Morgan sat down on the walk and pulled off his

boots and wool socks. The boots were hand made and
cost him 40 dollars. He was not about to get them all
muddied up just to teach manners to some drunken
cowboy.

In his bare feet he stepped down into the mire and
advanced to meet the other man. They assumed the
hands-on-shoulders position and began wrestling
around. No self-respecting man would hit anybody with
his fists.

The cowboy's weight advantage was soon apparent
as he threw Morgan backwards into the mud and
horseshit. However, he didn't have the wrestling experience to go with his weight, and when he tried to
dive on top, Morgan rolled to one side and let the cowboy land face-first in the slop.

The fight was over in less than three minutes. All
the hours of wrestling with his brother when they were
youngsters had taught Morgan some unbeatable holds.
He locked the cowboy into a full Nelson, and the man
either had to cry uncle or suffocate in the foul-smelling
mud. He cried uncle.

Morgan stood back and let the man pull himself up.
"Now you can just bring the lady's buggy around like
she asked you."

Rubbing the back of his neck, the cowboy slogged
across to the other side of the street where his friends
waited dejectedly. When he was safely out of reach he
called, "Get it yourself," and took off up the street
with the other two.

Morgan did not press the issue. He had clearly
beaten the man, and there was nothing to be gained by
insisting on an apology. What was more, there was always the possibility that the cowboy might change his
mind about risking gunplay.

He wiped the mud from his face with his sleeve,

which did little good, since the sleeve was just as muddy. The girl was still standing on the boardwalk, watching him with those wondrous eyes. "I'll have your rig around there in a jiffy," he said.

He plowed across the quagmire of the street, took hold of the horse's reins, and led the animal in a U back around to the front of the dry goods store where it was originally hitched.

The girl gave him a dazzling smile. "I truly thank you, Mr. . . ."

"Bunker's the name. Morgan Bunker. And don't mention it. I was lookin' for a little exercise."

When she heard his name a peculiar look flashed over the girl's face, but she did not grow any less friendly. "I'm Beth Catlin. I'm staying up at the Regal Hotel with my mother."

Morgan hoisted himself up onto the walk beside her. "Pleased to meet you." He glanced up at the buggy seat. "I'd offer to give you a lift up, but as you can see I got myself a mite grubby, and it'd be a shame to muddy up your dress and all."

"Oh, don't worry about that. I've got plenty more dresses at home."

Beth Catlin held out her arms to him. Morgan hesitated for a second, then swept her up off the walk and into the seat of the buggy. She weighed almost nothing, but she was plainly a woman where she had leaned against him during the transfer.

"I hate to leave you here with your clothes all wet and muddy like that," she said. "Especially since it's sort of my fault that you got that way."

"This is nothin'," Morgan said. "I been lots dirtier than this plenty of times."

"All the same, I feel bad about it." The girl's face brightened as though she'd had an inspiration. "Tell you what, you come on up to our room in the Regal and I'll rinse those things out for you and dry 'em over the stove. It won't take any time at all."

"Won't your ma be sorta concerned about you waltzin' in with some grubby stranger off the street?"

"My mother will be out now, attending to some of her business," said Beth. "Besides, I don't think you're exactly a stranger any more."

Morgan wondered about the strange emphasis Beth put on her last remark, but he did not wonder long. He was beginning to shiver with the cold under his wet clothes. More than that, he was feeling a pleasant ache down low in his belly at the thought of spending an hour or so with this firm-bodied, big-eyed girl. He said, "Well, if you're sure it won't discommode you any . . ."

"Are you going to stand down there jawing and shivering for another hour, or are you going to climb up here with me?" she said.

Morgan grinned at her. "I'm comin' up." He swung himself up and settled down on the padded seat beside her.

On the short ride up the main street to the Regal Hotel Morgan found himself talking with amazing ease to the girl. He told her things about himself he never thought anybody would be interested in. However, Beth Catlin asked just the right questions. She also looked at him in a way that made it seem like the story of his life was the most fascinating thing she had ever heard.

They got a good deal of attention from the people along the street, this fine-looking, well-dressed young girl and the grubby young man. The looks were slightly disapproving from the women, envious from the men. Morgan was enjoying himself hugely.

"Riding for the Pony Express must be about the

most exciting job in the world for a man," Beth said as they pulled to a stop in front of her hotel. "I guess they must be awful choosy about who they sign up."

"I reckon it is an honor of sorts," Morgan admitted. " 'Course, I had the jump on most of the boys who applied for the job, seein' as I was already employed by the Russell outfit."

"I'll bet they would have taken you anyway," Beth said, leaning close to him.

For a moment Morgan was almost overpowered by the crisp scent of clean young woman mixed with the tang of soap. "It's nice of you to say so," he managed to mumble.

Beth led him into the hotel through the lobby, ignoring the stares from the man behind the desk and the other people standing about. They went on up the stairs and she let them into the room with her key.

Morgan stepped inside and noted with some disappointment that Beth carefully left the door open the twelve inches that was required by propriety. He was ashamed of himself for having had some unworthy thoughts about the young lady. If he stopped to study on it, she clearly wasn't that kind.

"You can get behind the screen over by the other bed and take your clothes off," she said. "Pass them out to me and I'll have them cleaned up in a jiffy. At least enough so you'll look presentable. And smell a whole lot better," she added with a giggle.

Morgan did as he was told, stripping off his coat, shirt, and trousers, and folded them across the top of the screen. They were immediately snatched away by Beth. He was pleased that he'd kept the boots high and dry.

"Where's your longjohns?" Beth called from the other side of the screen.

"Say what?" Morgan was not sure he'd heard right.

"Your longjohns. Don't tell me you aren't wearing any?"

" 'Course I'm wearing 'em," Morgan said. What kind of a saddle tramp did she think he was?

"Well, hand 'em over. We might as well clean up the whole kaboodle while we're at it."

"They didn't get very dirty," Morgan said.

"Still they must have got wet. Hand 'em over."

"But then I'll have nothin' to wear."

"Wrap a blanket around yourself if you have to. Mercy, nobody's going to be looking at you."

Feeling embarassed and excited at the same time, Morgan peeled off the long underwear and laid it gingerly on top of the screen. He flinched when Beth whipped it off at once. He wondered how much could be seen through the cracks between panels of the screen. Quickly he grabbed a blanket off the bed and draped it around his body, covering as much of himself as he could.

This Beth Catlin was not like any girl he had known before. She sure wasn't the rough kind who'd drop her bloomers quick as a wink for a romp in the hay. But she wasn't one of them snooty females who came out from the east and looked at every man west of the Appalachians like he belonged in a cage. Morgan couldn't figure her out at all, but he knew he liked the feeling he got from being around her.

Morgan sat down on the bed all wrapped up like an Indian. He could hear the sounds of water being poured from the pitcher into the basin, and a scrub brush working on his clothes. Then there was a low hissing as Beth draped his wet clothes over the stove.

"You said your ma had some business to take care of?" he said to make conversation.

"That's right."

"What sort of business is she in?"

"Freight hauling."

"I declare, that sorta puts her and me in the same line of work. In a manner of speakin'."

"I s'pose you could say it does," Beth answered. There was a note of mischief in her voice that puzzled him. "Are you going to be around St. Joe long?" she asked.

"Nope. I'll be headin' out tomorrow early for Utah Territory."

"It's a shame you won't be staying here for a little while longer."

"I'm commencin' to think that myself," Morgan said.

After a moment Beth said, "Do you think the Pony Express will really work? I hear they expect to deliver mail from here to Sacramento in less than two weeks."

"Ten days is what Mr. Russell promised," Morgan said proudly. "And you can bet we'll do our damndest, excuse me, our darndest to keep him an honest man."

"That will surely take some doing," Beth said. "The best time the Butterfield outfit ever made with the mail to California over the southern route was 29 days."

"You know a powerful lot about the mail business for a girl," Morgan said. "Your pa must have somethin' to do with it."

"My pa was a gambler," Beth said. "Still is, as far as I know. He's long gone."

"Sorry," Morgan said. "I didn't mean to pry into what's none of my business."

"I don't mind," she told him. "I hardly knew the man. Ma got married right away again to a man with a couple of freight wagons. He died some five years back, and Ma's been runnin' the business ever since."

"That's mighty interestin'. What might be the name of your ma's second husband? Mayhap I'd know of him."

Beth peeked around the corner of the screen, her blue eyes dancing with mischief. "Mayhap you would," she said. "The name's McKee."

Morgan snatched at the blanket which had started to slip away. "Sam McKee from down K.C. way? You're Jessie McKee's daughter?"

"I am," she said impishly.

"Well, why in tarnation didn't you say so? And do you have to keep lookin' around the screen like that?"

"You are the bashful one, aren't you." Beth looked him over for another moment, then withdrew. "I didn't know it would make any difference who my mother is."

" 'Course it makes a difference. I mean, in a way it does. I work for Russell, Majors and Waddell, and they don't speak at all kindly of your ma or the Ace Freighters."

"I don't suppose they do," Beth said, "being business rivals the way they are."

"And then there's . . . well, there's my pa and your ma," Morgan said lamely.

"I know all about that. What's any of this got to do with you and me?"

"Well, nothin', I guess," Morgan stammered. "Say, what about you and me, anyway?"

Beth's answer was cut off by a new voice from the other side of the screen.

"What the Sam Hill's goin' on in here?"

"Mama, you're back early."

"Whose duds are those hanging over my stove?"

There was the clump of purposeful footsteps across the carpet, and the screen shielding Morgan was slapped to one side. Jessie McKee, green eyes ablaze, stood glaring at him.

"Howdy, Miz McKee."

"Don't howdy me, you son of a Bunker. What are you doing in my daughter's room naked?"

Morgan clutched the blanket more closely around him. "I ain't naked, Miz McKee."

"I don't want your sass, I want an explanation!"

Beth appeared behind her mother. "He got himself all muddied up whilst fighting a cowboy who was ragging me, Mama, so I asked him to come on up and let me clean up his clothes for him. We had the door open the whole time."

"I hope to kiss an Injun you did," Jessie said. "I ain't got enough trouble with the Bunkers. The old man's trying to drink the town dry and young Jack talks about leaving my outfit and goin' to work for that thievin' Russell bunch, and now I got the other one sniffin' around my daughter."

"Nothin' disrespectful happened between us," Morgan said. "My word on that."

"It better not," Jessie said. "I got ways of finding out." She held out a hand to her daughter. "Come on, Beth, you and me are leavin' this room for ten minutes, and when we come back there better be no sign of this Pony rider or I'll call in somebody who can handle the situation better than a couple of helpless females."

"Been nice meeting you, Morgan," Beth said from behind her mother.

"Likewise," he said.

Jessie made an exasperated sound, grabbed her daughter, and stalked out of the room.

When he was sure the women were gone, Morgan threw off the blanket and took down his clothes from where Beth had hung them over the stove. They were still a little damp, but in a whole lot better condition then when he walked in. He dressed quickly and took at last look around the room.

"I got a hunch we'll meet again, Beth Catlin," he said to the four walls. "And the sooner, the better, says I."

Whistling a jig through his teeth, he walked out and and floated down the stairs.

6

MORGAN Bunker went to bed early, but he found it nigh impossible to sleep. Not only was tomorrow the start of his new adventure with the Pony Express, there were the thoughts of blue-eyed Beth Catlin dancing through his head. He remembered the excitement he'd felt standing naked under the blanket with only the Chinese screen between him and the girl. If Beth had taken a close look right about then, not even the heavy blanket would have concealed the way he felt about her.

Morgan groaned and rolled over onto his stomach. He knew it wasn't healthy to have these kinds of thoughts, but he couldn't seem to think about anything else.

It was like the time when he lived on his uncle's farm in Boonville and was fooling around regular with the Pryor sisters. They were two and three years older than young Morgan at the time, and were more than willing to teach him how to use what he had. He had lived in an agony of guilt for weeks, but it never kept him from wandering over toward the Pryor place when his chores were done and he was feeling horny.

The way he felt about Beth Catlin was different. And yet it was the same. He would never think of doing anything disrespectful with her, but still she gave him twitches and aches in the damnedest parts of his body.

He wished Jack would show up so he could talk to his brother about it. Not that he would tell Jack everything, but sometimes it was good just to have another feller to talk to. Jack kept his own counsel a lot, and Morgan was not sure how worldly his brother was in these matters. He wished again that he could be closer to his brother.

As for the old man, Morgan didn't expect to see him until close to daylight. And even if he was here, Morgan could never share his feelings with Cherokee Joe. In a way, though, his feelings for Beth Catlin brought him closer to his father. After all, the old man was surely rolling Beth's mother in the hay now and again.

Morgan made a fierce effort to drag his thoughts away from the blonde girl. If he couldn't get his mind on something else, he'd start abusing himself, and they said that made you crazy.

He flipped back over onto his back and thought about his earliest memories, back when his mother was still alive. Elvira Bunker came from solid Missouri farming people. She had, in fact, brought with her a nice parcel of bottom land as a dowry when she married Cherokee Joe. Sadly, Joe turned out to be no shakes at all as a farmer, and it seemed to Morgan that the bank was always threatening to take over the Bunker place.

Perhaps mercifully, Elvira Bunker died of a fever before she saw her farm go completely to ruin. Cherokee Joe immediately gave up all pretense at working the land and went into a trade he was better suited for—holding up stagecoaches.

He kept the boys with him for about a year, during which they were always on the go, a jump ahead of the law. Morgan and Jack thought it was an exciting life, and never gave much thought to what their father did when he rode off with the other rough-looking men. As far as the boys knew theirs was a normal life, until the day the posse rode in at dawn and surrounded their cabin.

While Cherokee Joe was in prison Morgan and Jack lived with their mother's brother Henry and his wife outside of Boonville. Uncle Henry and Aunt Lil were getting along in years, and were not real happy about taking a couple of rambunctious nephews in to live with them. But there was no place else for the boys to go, and they were treated decent enough, even given a certain amount of schooling. In return, the boys did the work of a couple of hired hands around the farm, and had little time for skylarking. When Cherokee Joe got out of prison and came to take his boys back, the move suited everybody.

By that time Joe had met up with the Widow McKee. Although it was unclear to the boys just what kind of work he was doing for her, at least he wasn't breaking any laws. Jessie offered both of the boys a job with Ace Freighters. Jack took her up on it, but Morgan figured it was time he did something on his own, so he went off and got himself hired by the Central Overland.

It worried Morgan sometimes now that when his father got to drinking heavy he might be tempted to return to his old outlaw ways. Even more he worried about Jack. The boy didn't show a whole lot of gumption, and if Cherokee Joe went bad again, he just might pull his younger son along with him.

Just before he fell into an uneasy sleep Morgan wondered what was keeping Jack out so uncommon late.

Young Jack Bunker was busy that night learning how all-fired easy it was to spend ten dollars. He started out by passing up the Singletree Saloon in the center of town. He did not want to risk running into his father. Anyhow, the usual crowd at the Singletree seemed a mite quiet for what Jack had in mind for tonight. He headed instead for the Excelsior down alongside the Hannibal & St. Joseph tracks. There the action was continuous and loud.

He edged his way in through the roistering crowd and up to the bar. It was his intention to order a beer, having but small acquaintance with hard liquor. However, when he looked around and saw nobody else at the bar with a brew, he called for a glass of whiskey.

The first gulp he took of the liquor was much too big and it made his eyes water. He covered up the display of weakness by faking a coughing fit. Better to be thought consumptive than not man enough to handle a shot of redeye.

Jack took his time and was more careful with the second swallow. It went down lots smoother, but it still tasted like horse piss.

The pervading smell of the Excelsior Saloon was cigar smoke and sweat. Jack was suddenly aware that something behind him was smelling a whole lot sweeter. He turned around, a mite unsteady on his feet, and saw a woman standing there. She had a pile of curls on her head, very red lips, and a chest that bulged nicely over the top of her dress.

" 'Evenin', cowboy," she said in a husky voice. "Feelin' lonely?"

Jack tried to answer and was embarrassed to have

his voice go all squeaky and out of control. All that came out was a croak, which the woman took as an invitation to join him.

"My name's Lillian," she said. "How'd you like to buy me a drink?"

"I had an aunt by that name," Jack got out finally.

"Well, that sorta makes us pals already, don't it?" She elbowed him playfully in the ribs. "Long as you don't start treatin' me like your aunt."

"Oh, no, you ain't nothin' like her," Jack explained.

"I'll bet I ain't." Lillian signalled to the bartender. He came over with another glass, and this time left the bottle. He took some more of Jack's money away with him.

After that the level in the bottle went down surprisingly fast, and Jack was feeling just fine. After the first couple of drinks Jack found he had no trouble at all talking to Lillian. In a deep, he-man voice, at that. Or so it sounded to his ears. And from the way she laughed at everything he said, Jack figured he must be pretty amusing into the bargain. He even noticed some of the people standing around looking over and grinning in his direction. He grinned back at them and kept tossing down the whiskey. Wonderful stuff.

When the bottle was getting close to empty Lillian reached down and put her hand on him where no woman had ever touched. Instinctively Jack flinched away from her.

"What's the matter, honey?" Lillian said. "You got nothin' to be ashamed of down there."

Jack got all confused. Suddenly the whiskey didn't help him find the right words.

"I, uh . . . well, I, uh . . ."

"Don't tell me you're bashful? A handsome-lookin' young buck like you?"

"Shoot, no, I ain't bashful."

"I didn't think so." She rubbed him down there, and this time Jack held his ground. "I'll bet you've pleasured many a girl in your time."

"Uh, there's been one or two, I reckon." The truth was that Jack Bunker had never so much as seen a girl without her clothes on, let alone pleasured any of them. But damned if he was going to let on.

"You want to go out back with me?" Lillian said, giving him a little squeeze.

"Out back?" His damn voice was squeaking again.

"I got a crib out there. Real cozy-like."

"Oh, sure." Jack made an effort to focus his eyes, which seemed to be wandering around aimlessly. "How much?" It was time to make it clear he knew what was going on here.

"Don't worry about it, honey," Lillian said. "You got plenty."

"Okay, let's go," Jack croaked. He made a grab for the whiskey bottle but missed and knocked it off the bar. He bent down to retrieve the bottle and almost fell on his face.

Lillian grabbed him by the elbow and tugged him back upright. "We don't need that firewater, honey. Come along with Lillian."

They went through a store room in the rear of the saloon and out the back door. Jack hung on to Lillian as they walked. He wondered why they hadn't leveled the path back here.

Out behind the saloon was a long shed that had once been a stable. Now it was partitioned off into half a dozen tiny rooms that the working girls rented from the owner of the Excelsior. Jack heard shrieks of female laughter and male guffaws coming from the occupied cribs. There were other sounds he could not identify.

Lillian propped Jack against the rough wooden wall while she pushed open the door to her crib. With her help he lurched inside.

The air was heavy with the smell of humanity and cheap perfume. Jack belched loudly.

" 'Scuse me," he said.

"Do you like it with the lamp lit or in the dark?" Lillian asked.

"Huh?" he replied.

"We'll do it in the light," Lillian decided. "That makes it friendlier, don't you think?"

"Huh?"

She struck a match and touched it to the wick of a coal oil lamp that stood on an upended wooden crate. The only other thing in the room was a cot with cowhide stretched over a wooden frame. The cot was covered by a crusty old blanket.

The oily smell of the lamp flame combined with the other odors in the airless room to make Jack's stomach turn over. He clenched his jaw and squinted his eyes, trying to make the floor stop tilting.

Lillian perched on the cot. She spread her knees apart and hoisted her skirts. Jack gawked like some fool hay shoveler on his first trip to town. He had no idea women had so much hair down there.

"Come on, honey," she said, "let's don't waste time. It gets cold out here."

Jack tried to speak, but his voice was completely gone now. He had to keep swallowing a sour lump of something that wanted to rise in his throat.

Lillian looked at him curiously. "You gonna get them britches down?"

Jack wobbled toward her.

"Steady there, son." She put out a hand to keep him from toppling across the cot and banging his head on the wall. "I guess you could use a little help."

She undid his belt buckle and deftly opened the buttons on the front of his pants. Jack stared down at her as though watching this happening to somebody else.

When his pants were open Lillian pushed them down around his knees and started on the lower buttons of his union suit. She reached in and grasped his genitals.

Jack mumbled something, being unable to form words with his numb lips.

"Looks like we're gonna have to work on this a little, honey," Lillian said. She leaned forward and did something Jack had never thought possible for a woman, even a whore. She took him in her mouth.

That was the last thing he remembered until he awoke on a pallet back in the storeroom of the Excelsior. His head hurt like fury, and his stomach roiled around like there was a nest of snakes inside.

He staggered to his feet, checked to see that he had all his clothes on, then staggered out through the back door and puked. He felt some better then, but he was in no mood to walk back through the saloon and face all those grinning men, and above all Lillian. His ten dollars was gone, but that was no matter. He figured he must have got his money's worth. When his head felt better he would try to recollect just what all happened out there in the crib, then he would have a right good story to tell. But right now all he wanted to do was go somewhere and lie down. He stumbled off in the direction of the hotel where he had a room with his father and his brother.

7

ABOUT the time his younger son was learning about
life's mysteries from a whore named Lillian, Cherokee
Joe Bunker was climbing the stairs at the Regal Hotel.
He was bathed and shaved, and had even paid a dollar
to a Chinaman to have his clothes cleaned up. He
passed up the front room where Jessie McKee was
staying with her daughter, and went on to a smaller
room the widow took for her after-hours business. He
knocked on the door and walked in without waiting for
an invitation.

Although the room was smaller and did not have the
window overlooking the street, it was just as richly fur-
nished as the other one. The bed, with the comforter
already turned back, had a pair of plump down pillows
and real linen sheets.

Jessie herself was sitting on the end of the bed. She
was wearing something black and silky that tied in the
front. Her hair was brushed down around her shoulders, all soft and shiny.

"You're late," she said.

"You said you wanted me all cleaned up."

Jessie sniffed at the air. "What's that smell?"

"Toilet water. Came all the way from Paris, France. So the barber said."

"Wherever it comes from, it's an improvement," Jessie said.

Joe strode across the room to where Jessie was sitting. He grabbed her by the elbows, pulled her up, and kissed her hard on the mouth.

Jessie struggled against him, and finally pulled her head back. "Couldn't we at least sit down and talk a little first?"

"What for? We ain't got nothin' to talk about that's so important it can't wait till afterwards."

"God, you're romantic," she said.

"You don't want romance, woman. You want what I got hangin' between my legs, and you know it. Now why don't you just shuck that thing you're wearin' and get yourself into that bed."

Jessie squirmed out of his grasp and stepped away. She looked at him sideways. "What if I told you I wasn't in the mood tonight?"

"First I'd tell you that's a load of bullshit, then I'd rip that thing off you and throw you down and fuck you till you squealed."

"Do you think you're man enough to do all that?"

"We'll Goddamn well find out in a hurry." Joe made a lunge for her and grabbed the collar of the silky wrap. Jessie spun away from him and the wrap slipped off her shoulders easily and hung in Joe's hand. He stood for a moment just looking at her.

"Jesus, for a woman your age, you got a helluva body on you, Jessie."

"Thirty-four ain't exactly ready for the rocking chair. And what about you? You gotta be forty."

"Mebbe so, but I can still get it up better'n most young scalawags. As you oughta know."

"Oh, I will admit you're hung fair to middlin'," she taunted.

"Better'n that, woman." Joe made a grab for her, but she danced naked out of his reach. "Just you stand still for a minute and I'll show you who's hung and who ain't."

"Jesus, you're crude as dirt."

"And you love it."

"Do I?"

"You know damn well you do."

Joe lunged for her again, and again Jessie slipped away.

"All right, Goddamn it, that's enough fartin' around for one night. Get your ass on that bed and get your legs in the air."

"Make me."

"You think I can't?"

Jessie's eyes sparkled as she looked him up and down. "I wonder."

"I know what you need. You need that perky little backside tanned."

Joe's hand shot out, and this time Jessie was a fraction slow in getting out of the way. His hand clamped hard on her wrist.

"Oh, no Joe," she cried, "you're not going to do that to me?"

"Oh, ain't I? When you act like a teasin' little brat, you're gonna get treated like one. C'mere."

Joe sat down heavily on the bed and yanked Jessie around so she fell across his lap with her pale bare bottom looking up at him. Holding her there with his left hand, he brought his right hand down hard, palm first, flat across the crease of her ass.

"Ow!" she screeched. "Jesus, that hurts!"

Whack!

"Ow, Joe, stop it."

Whack!

"Please, Joe, not so hard!"

Whack!

"God, Joe, don't!"

Whack!

"Oh, yes!"

Whack!

"Again!"

Whack!

"More! Harder!"

Joe gave her a last swat on the rump and yanked her to her feet. "That's all of that we're gonna do tonight. I got some other plans for you."

He spun her around and pushed her down face first on the bed. Her bare knees rested on the floor. Her buttocks, now glowing a rosy pink, were raised and ready for him. He unbuckled and dropped his pants, taking his time getting out of his clothes.

Jessie stayed where she was, bent forward over the bed. She peeked back at him through a curtain of red hair.

"Hurry up, Joe. Do it to me. Fuck me good. Fuck me real good, darlin'."

8

THE next morning at first light Morgan Bunker stood on the wooden sidewalk outside the Central Overland stage depot with Bolivar Roberts and three other men. A gleaming red stagecoach with gold trim and gold tracery around the door panel stood waiting in the road. The six horses pawed nervously at the dirt and snorted steam in the chilly morning air. The driver was already aboard, and the men's gear had been stowed in the boot on the back end of the coach.

Roberts introduced Morgan to the three other passengers. They were all being sent out to their new jobs as station keepers along the Pony Express route. Morgan felt honored to be the only rider being carried west by the special stage. As each man stepped up into the coach, Roberts shook his hand and wished him luck. When they were all inside Morgan expected them to get rolling, but the driver sat tight while Roberts paced the platform, checking his watch and peering off up the road.

After they had been all loaded and ready to go for ten minutes, the passengers started getting itchy. Then

Roberts heaved a big sigh and put his watch away as a
horse and buggy from the livery stable came clopping
down the street. There was a driver and one passenger.
At the stage landing the passenger got out and lifted a
new-looking carpetbag out with him. He was a tall man
with wide shoulders and no hips. He had a luxurious
black moustache and eyes like bullets.

Bolivar Roberts greeted the man formally. Then he
opened the door and leaned into the stage.

"Gentlemen, this is Captain Jack Slade. He's signed
on as line supervisor for the Pony. He'll be riding all
the way through to Sacramento so as to be there when
our first rider brings the mail in."

There were mumbled greetings from the four men in
the coach, but the easy chatter of a few minutes before
died when the newcomer climbed in. The name of Jack
Slade was well known along the frontier since the Mexican War twelve years earlier. No one seemed to know
if he came by the rank of Captain officially or if he had
pinned it on himself. And nobody was about to question him on it. Jack Slade had the reputation of being
right handy with a pistol, and not a bit bashful about
proving it. "Mean" was the word most often used to
describe him, especially when he was into the liquor.

He was sober this morning, and seemed personable
enough as he nodded to the three station keepers and
took the seat beside Morgan. Slade was dressed better
than the rest of them in a black frock coat, string tie,
and a broad-brimmed planter's hat. It seemed to Morgan a mite fancy for cross-country travel, but if that's
the way Jack Slade wanted to dress, so be it.

The driver yelled at the horses and they lurched forward in unison against their collars. With a creak of
wood, the snap of leather, and a jingle and clink, the
stage leaped forward.

All along the main street of St. Joe early risers waved and whistled as the gleaming stagecoach rumbled past. Morgan craned out the window when they went past the Regal Hotel, trying to see the second floor, just in case Beth Catlin might be looking out. There might have been a blonde head there behind a curtain, but from his angle he could not be sure.

In no time at all they were out of St. Joseph and heading west through the Kansas prairie. The coach was one of the new Concord models with the body suspended on layered straps of tough steer hide. These were fast replacing the old spine-jolting Holladays. Over the ruts and bumps of the Western roads the Concord coach gave a gentle pitching, rolling ride that was about as comfortable a way as there was for a man to travel.

Since there were only five passengers, the center seat was folded down so they all had plenty of room and didn't have to get their legs tangled up. Jack Slade didn't have much to say, but kept to himself, watching out the side window with those bullet eyes. After a while the others loosened up and began to talk among themselves. The station men were a few years older than Morgan, and their jobs would not carry the glamor of his, but they all felt a strong kinship in being a part of the new venture.

With the light load and gentle weather all the way, the stagecoach made good time. Three days out of St. Joseph they dropped the first station keeper off at Fort Kearney. At the end of a week they left the second keeper at Laramie, and the third a day later at Fort Bridger.

Morgan Bunker and Jack Slade rode on as the only passengers. Slade was still disinclined to talk, and Morgan respected his wishes. When he felt like company he would climb up next to the driver, a long-jawed man named Polk who had a thousand stories of his adventures driving both for the Central Overland and Butterfield. About half the stories were plain lies, but the man told them so well it didn't make any difference.

At dawn on the morning after they dropped the Fort Bridger man off, Morgan was jolted out of a sleep by shouts and the sound of gunfire close by. By the time the coach swayed to a stop Morgan was fully awake and scrambling for his pistol. Jack Slade was already crouched at the window with a revolver in each hand.

"What's goin' on?" Morgan whispered.

Slade silenced him with a shake of his head.

From out in the morning twilight came the muffled voice of a man. "Throw down the box, driver."

"Ain't no box," Polk called from his high seat. "This here's a special run."

"You better not be lyin' or you're a dead man."

"Look for yourself," Polk said.

By flattening himself in the rear corner of the coach Morgan could see a mounted man up front by the horses. He wore his kerchief pulled up over his nose. Morgan started to raise his pistol but Slade motioned him back.

There was a jiggling and banging as somebody climbed up and yanked open the chest under the driver's seat where the strongbox was usually kept.

"He's tellin' the truth," said a new voice from up top. "It's empty."

"Try the boot," said the first voice.

Spurs jingled and feet scraped across the roof of the stage as the man climbed back from the driver's perch to the leather boot at the rear. From inside Morgan could hear him unbuckle the straps and poke through the contents.

"Ain't nothin' back here but a couple of worthless carpetbags."

The mounted man up front swore. "All right, passengers out. Drop the gunbelts first, then come out grabbin' the sky."

Morgan looked to Slade. The tall captain signalled him with his eyes to stay calm. He shoved his guns back into their holsters, unbuckled the belt, and dropped it out the window. Morgan did the same, but reluctantly. He did not like surrendering to bandits, and he was disappointed in his traveling companion.

Jack Slade stepped out of the coach first, his hands in the air. Morgan followed, and as he reached the ground a terrible thought hit him. The voices of both the road agents had been muffled by their kerchiefs. Wouldn't it be a hell of a note if Cherokee Joe had lapsed into his old habits and was now holding up his own son?

As soon as he could see both of the men, Morgan relaxed a little. One of them had bushy red eyebrows and the other a hanging belly. Neither of the men was his father.

"Stand easy, gents," said the mounted man with the eyebrows. "You'll be on your way again soon as we relieve you of some of that extra weight."

He nodded to the man with the belly, who started going through Slade's pockets. Morgan glanced around to get the lay of the land. Behind the two outlaws was a thick grove of cottonwoods where they had probably been waiting. On the far side of the road was a cutbank that rose a couple of feet higher than the top of the stage. There was no place for a man to run, even if he was of a mind to.

The fat road agent pulled a fancy engraved gold watch from Slade's pocket and yanked the other end of the chain loose.

"What have we got here?" he said, popping the case open.

"The timepiece has a sentimental value to me," Slade said. "I'll ask you politely to return it."

The two outlaws stared at him for a moment, then turned to each other and started laughing fit to kill.

"Sentimental value," said the one who had taken the watch. "Ain't that the damndest thing you ever heard from a grown-up man?"

While they were still laughing Jack Slade kind of stretched his right arm a little, and like magic his hand was filled with one of the new Remington double-barreled derringers. He fired once and the .41-caliber slug punched the fat man in the middle of the chest, knocking him backward. While he was still going down Slade fired the second barrel and put a black hole above the mounted outlaw's left eye.

As the two road agents thudded to the dirt Morgan caught a shadow of movement on the bank across the road.

"Behind you!" he yelled.

Slade dove for the ground where he'd dropped his gunbelt. Up on the bank a pistol barked. The slug kicked up gravel where Slade had just been standing. He rolled over, came up with a Colt in his fist, and put three bullets into the third bandit while the first was still in his dying twitches.

When he found his voice again Morgan said, "Captain Slade, that was as fancy a piece of shooting as I ever hope to see."

Slade stood up and brushed the road dust from his clothes. "It was mostly luck," he said. "And if you hadn't warned me, that hombre up there behind us would have ended my shooting days forever." He buckled his guns back on, retrieved his watch from the dead man, and said to the driver, "If the horses are settled down, I suggest we get rolling."

Polk swallowed hard and said, "Right, Captain."

Morgan and Slade climbed back inside, the driver yelled "Heeyah!" at the horses, and the stage lurched on westward.

9

IN the northeast corner of the young Colorado Territory the town of Julesburg was a hustling, roistering stage junction. Leaving Julesburg, part of the traffic continued west through Utah Territory toward California. The rest turned south for Pike's Peak and Denver.

The social center of Julesburg was the Buckskin Saloon and Card Club. It was here that Smiler Tate and two companions rested at a rear table after many days on the trail from St. Joseph. They were tired and dirty, and drank thirstily from the foaming glasses of beer in front of them.

The three men sat in a corner isolated from the noisy activity around them. The other two appeared to be waiting for Smiler to speak, but he only stared darkly into his beer. Finally one of the others, a broken-nosed gunman with a shock of curly hair, cleared his throat.

"Uh, how much farther you figure we'll have to go, Smiler?"

"No farther. This is where we do it."

"Well, thank the Lord. I was commencin' to think

" Reni laughed again. "But we can still
together. Just you and me."
ked across the table at the other two men.
on up to the bar."
Pete pushed their chairs back with con-
ctance.
artender whatever you order is on Jules,"
aan.
nk you, Mr. Reni," said Curly, and the
moved off toward the bar with sudden en-

a small signal with a forefinger. A bottle
to the table and two drinks poured. He
and they both drank.
es you to find Jules Reni working for the
?"
t," Smiler admitted. "There's stories
ow you ain't completely ignorant about
tage holdups around here."
ard those stories myself. Damn my eyes if
they come from."

h stories were true, the Central Overland
y wise to hire Jules Reni to manage this

you mean."
tend to earn the money they pay me.
eni is in charge, there will be no holdups
my district, and the Pony Express riders
passage through Julesburg." Reni paused
ver, bringing his face close to Smiler's.
at happens to these people once they are
rict, that is not my concern."
get you," Smiler said. "The problem for

we were gonna ride clear to California to get an open
shot at a Pony rider."

"Maybe you think you oughta be headin' up this
party instead of me?"

"It ain't that, it's just that me and Pete are itchin' to
get on with the business." He turned to the third man
at the table, a young Texan with a bad case of pimples.
"Ain't that so, Pete?"

Pete nodded.

Smiler gave them a hard look. "Hell, do you think I
like bein' all the way out here any better than you do?
No tellin' what that polecat Cherokee Joe Bunker will
talk the Widow McKee into while I'm not there."

The other two men looked at each other quickly, but
said nothing.

Smiler caught the exchange, and his eyes darkened.
"I studied the land as we rode in, and there's a place
on the trail east of town where the trees crowd right
down to the road on both sides. You can't see a blame
thing from the trail, and from a little ways into the
trees, we can't miss."

Young Pete spoke up. "It's a good enough spot, all
right, but I still don't see why we had to ride all this
way. Why, we coulda sat right there in St. Joe and
waited for the first rider to saddle up, then rode out a
couple of miles, waited for him, and plugged him."

"Too risky," said Smiler. "When that first Pony
Express rider heads out it'll be big news in St. Joe. The
town'll be celebratin', and he'll likely have company all
the way to Marysville. By the time they get this far, we
know the man'll be ridin' alone. What's more, west of
Fort Kearney we don't have to worry much about the
law."

"Ain't this town got a marshal?" Curly asked.

"Nobody for us to worry about. The only law they

Lee Davis Willoughby

got here is a man named Jules Reni, and I heard he ain't the best of friends with the Central Overland."

"What's he gonna think about us holdin' pistol practice in his town?"

Smiler patted a leather pouch that was fastened to his belt. "The Widow McKee sent along this bag of gold to persuade people like Reni if we have to."

The other two men looked unconvinced.

"There's another reason why we got to nail the rider here," Smiler said. "I couldn't find out which trail west the Pony Express will take out of Julesburg. They could follow the North Platte up through Fort Laramie or take the south fork through Sterling. We got to do it here."

There was a stir among the other customers in the Buckskin. Smiler and his two companions turned toward the entrance. They saw a bear of a man with a huge moustache striding toward them. Curly and Pete shifted slightly in their chairs to make it easier to get at their guns.

The big man came to a stop at their table. " 'Allo, gentlemen," he said in a heavy French-Canadian accent. "I welcome you to Julesburg."

The men at the table eyed him suspiciously.

"I am Jules Reni."

"Howdy," said Smiler. "We've heard of you."

"Everybody has heard of Jules. You are the man called Smiler Tate?"

"That's right. How do you know me?"

"It is my business to know everything that happens in Julesburg." He indicated Curly and Pete with a nod of his head. "These are your men?"

"They're with me," Smiler said.

"If they are your friends, you will ask them to move their hands away from their pistols. A dozen men in

this room are ready
touches iron."

Smiler squinted ar
that Jules Reni spoke
Curly and Pete, and
on the table.

"Thank you," said
der his moustache. "M

Smiler pulled out th
down.

"What is it that
friends?"

Smiler eyed him cag
if you already knew th

"I did hear that it
Pony Express that con

"Maybe," Smiler ad

"I hear also that
chances of going throu

"Where would you
said.

"People say I have
ily for a moment, th
for you, my friend."

"Such as?"

The big man's vo
off the Pony Express

There was a str
"Maybe we could tal

Reni shook his
about. You see, I
Overland. In fact, I
in this district."

"You?" Smiler c

"Yes, m
have a drin

Smiler l

"You boys
Curly a
siderable r

"Tell th
said the bi

"Why,
two of the
thusiasm.

Reni ma
was broug
toasted Sn

"It surp
Pony Expr

"Somev
around as
some of th

"I have
I know wh

"Yeah."

"But if
might be v
district, no

"I see wh

"And I
While Jules
of stages in
will have sa
and leaned

"But as to v
out of my di

"I think

somebody who might be plannin' to, say, interfere with the Pony Express is that he'd have to know the route west of here if he was to pick a likely spot. The Central Overland people have been mighty close-mouthed about that."

"You can't blame them for that," Reni said.

"I suppose not."

"Of course, I, as district manager, have a copy of the complete route of the Pony Express from St. Joe to Sacramento, along with the locations of all stations and the names of the riders for each lap."

Smiler whistled through his teeth. "Somethin' like that would make mighty interestin' readin'. Any chance you might consider sellin' it?"

Reni spread his hands on the table. "I am, after all, a businessman."

Later that night around their campfire outside the town Smiler and his two companions studied the handwritten copy of the Pony Express route with the riders' names.

"How much did you have to pay the old thief for this?" Curly asked.

"Took everything the widow gave me," Smiler said.

"Too bad you couldn't have saved a little of that gold for the three of us," Pete complained.

Smiler's exposed teeth glinted in the firelight. He said, "Jules Reni is not the kind of a man you hold out on."

The three man bent closer to the sheet of paper in Smiler's hands.

"Appears they'll be followin' the North Platte," said Curly.

"I wouldn't want to do anything too close to Fort

Laramie," said Pete. "Not with all them soldiers around."

Smiler was running a finger down the list of the riders' names. "Say, Curly, doesn't Cherokee Joe have a couple of boys?"

"That's right. One of 'em, Jack, works for the widow. Still wet behind the ears, but he's a good worker. You know him, most prob'ly."

"What's the other one's name?"

"It's Morgan, if I recollect right. I do believe he works for the Central Overland."

"Morgan Bunker," Smiler repeated. He tapped a finger alongside the name on his list. "Boys, I just decided where we're gonna git us our Pony rider."

Curly and Pete looked to him expectantly.

"It's in the Utah Territory, out of a station called Three Fools Creek."

10

MORGAN Bunker's first look at the Pony Express station at Three Fools Creek was not encouraging. It consisted of a low adobe structure with a corral, surrounded by patchy scrub grass and sage brush at the base of the Shoshone Mountains. Off to the west in the direction of Carson City, there was alkali desert with towering saguaro cactuses spotted across the landscape like silent sentries.

Morgan swung down from the stage and retrieved his carpetbag from the boot. Capt. Jack Slade stepped out to shake his hand.

"Good luck to you, son."

"Thank you, Captain."

"It's been a memorable ride."

"That it has, sir. It was surely a pleasure meetin' up with you."

"Likewise. Maybe we'll get together again one of these days."

"I hope so."

Slade climbed back aboard. The driver yelled at the horses, and the stage clattered on toward California, raising a cloud of bitter alkali dust in its wake. Morgan watched it go, feeling like a marooned seaman.

The station keeper at Three Fools was a bandy-legged Irishman named Garrity. He walked with Morgan toward the station house, watching the expression on the younger man's face.

"Well, what do you think of your new home?"

"It's, uh, cozy-lookin'."

Garrity laughed. "That's a nice way of sayin' it's a Godforsaken spot on the Godforsaken desert, which is true enough. Howsomever, the place will look a lot better to you when you come in tired and hungry off the 120-mile ride from Carson City. We've got a Chinaman who can cook better'n most, and we get cool nights for sleepin' no matter how hot the day is."

They went inside and Morgan stowed his gear over the bunk Garrity told him would be his. He met Chops, the Chinese cook, and Wilson, the young wrangler.

"There'll be two or three more men here once the operation gets goin'," Garrity told him, "but for now, we're it."

"Can I see the horses?" Morgan asked.

"Sure."

Garrity and Wilson went with him back behind the station house to the corral. It was a round, white-washed affair with long wooden rails lashed to upright posts with rawhide. Inside the enclosure half a dozen horses browsed on the scrub grass. They were not the rangy, high-grade stock that had been selected for the stretches of prairie east of Fort Kearney. These were tough, stocky little mustangs, better suited to the hard deserts and steep mountain runs in the west.

Garrity reached up and scratched a bay gelding behind the ear. The animal shoved its muzzle inside the Irishman's coat looking for a treat.

"These fellers get treated even better than the riders," Garrity said. "They get a grain mixture sent all the way from Kansas City to go along with their grass forage. Healthiest critters you'll want to see. They'll go wherever you ask 'em, and they'll outrun anything on four legs. Treat your pony like your mother, boy. Your life will depend on him."

Garrity gave the nuzzling horse his sugar lump, and the three men walked back to the station house.

Morgan had two weeks to kill before he actually started his new job. The first rider was not scheduled to leave from St. Joseph for a week, and it would be another seven days before the first mail reached Three Fools Creek. Morgan spent much of the time riding back and forth over the route he would follow between his home station and Carson City. The Overland Trail in that section was about half hard-rock desert and half craggy ravines. Morgan rode over it slowly, taking note of possible shortcuts and looking out for danger spots that would provide poor footing for the horse.

Between Three Fools Creek and Carson City were four relay stations where Morgan would change horses. They were even smaller and grubbier than the home station, amounting to little more than an adobe hut and an enclosure for the horses. Morgan met the keeper and the wrangler at each of these stations. It was their job to have a fresh mount saddled and ready for him 30 minutes before he was scheduled to arrive. The mochila, a leather blanket with four locked mail compartments, would be swung from the back of the spent horse to the fresh one while Morgan relieved himself and maybe grabbed a biscuit to chew on the way. The entire relay operation was supposed to take no more than two minutes.

The days went by slowly, and Morgan was eager to hit the trail with his first mochila. He covered the ground he would ride over until he knew it like the south forty of his Uncle Henry's farm.

Once he saw a party of three Paiute braves watching him from a ridge well off to the north. He recalled the rule laid down by Bolivar Roberts—If you see one Indian be friendly, if you see two be careful, if you see three get ready to run. The job of the Pony Express was delivering the mail, not fighting Indians. The Paiutes watching Morgan made no move to come closer, so he kept to a steady, unhurried pace, keeping an eye on them until at last they wheeled and rode away.

The Paiutes were considered very bad medicine in the Utah Territory. It had not always been that way. After some early unpleasantness, the Paiutes seemed willing to live in peace with the Mormons, who were the first white men to move into the territory. The Mormons were hard-working and fair, and were ready to respect the Indians' hunting rights and their tribal customs. It was a different story with the Forty-Niners who streamed toward California for the gold. They looked on the Indians as something less than human, and would shoot them down for the plain hell of it. They even had rounded up the local Indians like animals and used them as slaves to wash out gold in the stream beds until the federal government put a stop to that. Needless to say, the feeling between the whites and the Paiutes by 1860 was one of dark distrust, with the threat of violence always smoldering just beneath the surface. So it was with some relief that Morgan saw the three braves ride off peaceably.

When he was not studying the trail between Three Fools and Carson City, Morgan killed time playing poker with Garrity, Wilson, and Chops. Since none of them would have any money until the first pay came through, they played for cartridges, known as cowboy change in the frontier towns. Chops won most of the time, relying on a canny, conservative style of play. The others didn't complain much, since when the cook was sulking he was likely to serve up burnt beans and gritty coffee. The card playing helped fill in the time, but for Morgan the day could not come too soon when he would start carrying the mail.

11

WHILE Morgan Bunker played cards and rode practice runs over the trail between Three Fools and Carson City, Smiler Tate and his two companions were covering the same ground. They followed the map purchased from Jules Reni, and were careful to stay out of sight of the relay stations. After the Pony rider met with his misfortune, it would not do to have somebody at one of the stations recall seeing three strangers riding through.

They made their camp at the foot of the Stillwater Mountains, well away from the usual traffic routes. Three days before Morgan's ride was scheduled to begin, Smiler and Pete hunkered around their fire and waited for the Arbuckles to boil while the eastern sky turned pink with the dawn.

Curly untangled himself from his bedroll and came over to join them. He stretched, making his joints pop.

"I'll be mighty glad to get back to sleepin' in a real bed," he said.

"When this job is done we can all take a week off

and live like kings in San Francisco," Smiler told him. "Beds and women as soft as you want."

"That sounds good to me," Pete agreed.

"Trouble is," Curly said, "we had to use all the gold the widow gave you to buy the map off that old thief Jules Reni."

"That was money well spent," Smiler said. "Besides, the Widow McKee will come through with plenty more once we nail that Pony rider."

"You picked out the place where we're goin' to do it?" Pete asked.

"Yep. The other side of Frenchman's Flats the trail runs through a dry ravine for near a quarter mile. Just under the head of the bluff there's a rock shelf where a man could wait and damn near poke the rider in the ear with a rifle barrel."

"I'll be glad when it's over and done with," Pete said.

Curly rubbed at his jaw. "One thing bothers me. When the rider doesn't show up at his next station, it won't be long before somebody comes lookin' for him."

"So they'll find a dead man," Smiler said.

"The Central Overland don't take kindly to havin' their men bushwhacked. Will we have time to clear out of the territory before they come after us?"

"I been studyin' on that problem," Smiler said, "and I think I got it solved."

"That so?"

"First, let's go take another look at the ravine."

After assuring themselves that the ledge over the ravine provided adequate cover for the ambush, Smiler led his men slowly west paralleling the trail. Suddenly he held up his hand, and they reined to a halt.

Up ahead of them, motionless, watching, were three mounted figures.

"Paiutes," Curly muttered. "Looks like the same ones we been seein' the last couple of days."

"They seem peaceable enough," said Pete, "but you can never be sure with redskins."

Smiler motioned them forward. "Follow me. And don't do anything sudden until I make my play."

"What are we gonna do?" Pete asked.

"We're gonna turn some live Injuns into some good Injuns."

Smiler rode slowly toward the Paiute party with the others flanking him. His eyes ranged over the surrounding countryside. There was no sign of other life, white man or Indian, in any direction.

The three Paiute braves had been sent to observe the unusual activity along the white man's trail, and to report back to their tribe any signs of hostility. Their orders were to avoid any confrontation. They were nearly convinced after more than a week of scouting that the white man's preparations along the trail were innocent of trouble for the Indians. They were, in fact, preparing to return to their village when the three white men approached.

Smiler noted that the three Paiute braves wore no war paint. They were dressed in buckskin shirts and breeches, with plain headbands and the usual pair of eagle feathers.

Smiler reined to a stop a few feet away, as did Curly and Pete on either side of him. He raised his right hand in the peace sign.

The brave who carried the rifle urged his pony forward to meet him. With their horses nose to nose, the Indian looked each of the white men over carefully. Then his own hand came up to return the greeting.

Instantly a revolver flashed up in Smiler's left hand. He fired at can't-miss range into the brave's chest.

"Run 'em down!" he shouted.

Curly and Pete brought their own guns into play. The Indians had no chance to reach for their bows and arrows before they were cut down.

The sudden fusillade echoed off the nearby mountains and the three Paiute braves lay in the dirt, darker now with blood. Their frightened ponies galloped off a short distance and stood pawing the ground nervously.

One of the braves groaned and began painfully to crawl toward the ponies. Smiler walked his horse over until he sat directly above the wounded Paiute. He took careful aim and fired one shot into the back of the man's head.

"Now they're three good Injuns," he said, wheeling around to face his companions.

"Not that it matters a whole lot," Curly said, reholstering his pistol, "but what did we gun the redskins down for?"

"I'll tell you a secret," Smiler said, "these Injuns ain't as dead as they look."

"What d'you mean?"

"In the next couple of days these three Paiutes are gonna be seen ridin' close to a couple of Pony Express stations lookin' all mean and sneaky. Then when the rider comes through Frenchman's Flats carryin' the mail, they're gonna dry gulch him."

"I don't follow you, Smiler," Curly said.

"Me neither," Pete chimed in.

Smiler took a look over his shoulder. "Pete, you come help me round up them ponies. Curly, you get down and pull the clothes off them braves."

The men stared at him. "Pull their clothes off?" Curly said.

"That's right. Get the headbands and feathers too. We can't look like proper Injuns without feathers."

"You want *us* to dress up like Injuns?"

"Now you got the idea. When they set out lookin' for whoever killed the Pony rider, people are gonna remember the three shifty Paiutes they seen skulkin' hereabouts."

"Hell, Smiler, even wearin' feathers and ridin' Injun ponies we don't look like no redskins," Pete said.

"We will if we don't get too close, and if we're never seen in the full light. Anyhow, they'll puzzle over it long enough for us to clear out of the territory."

"What about the Paiutes?" Curly said. "When they find three of their braves been murdered, they're gonna be plumb displeasured."

"That's nothin' to us. If they want to go on the war-path, let 'em. By the time they hold their council we'll be long gone to California."

"I hope you know what you're doin', Smiler," Curly said.

Smiler's eyes narrowed. The puckered lip drew even higher on the scarred side of his face. "Are you sayin' you got doubts about the way I'm handlin' this?"

"No doubts, Smiler," Curly said quickly. He swung down to the ground and looked with distaste at the three dead Indians.

"I'm glad to hear that," Smiler said. "Now hurry up and strip them redskins before the scorpions get at 'em."

Curly walked over to the three bodies. He squatted beside them and began to pull the bloody buckskin off one of the bodies. Smiler and Pete whirled off toward the spot where the three ponies huddled nervously.

12

On Tuesday April the third, Morgan Bunker paced restlessly around the station at Three Fools Creek trying to imagine the events taking place back in St. Joseph, where the first of the Pony Express riders was due to leave at four in the afternoon. It would be eight days before his own lap would be due, but Morgan would be with each of the riders in spirit every mile of the way. He had studied the schedule until he knew within a mile or so exactly where the mail should be at any time during the 180 scheduled hours between St. Joe and Three Fools.

Garrity the station keeper and Chops the cook avoided the jumpy young rider during his bouts of pacing. Wilson the wrangler patiently answered again and again Morgan's questions about the condition of the horses. They were all fit and ready to go.

Morgan had long since memorized the trail he would ride, so there would be little for him to do now, except wait for the blast of the horn that would signal the arrival of the rider from Camp Floyd whom he would replace. Meanwhile, he worried constantly that something would go wrong.

Actually, something *did* go wrong at the very start.

It was a day of celebration in St. Joe. The Pony Express gave people a welcome relief from grim talk of secession by the southern states, and speculation over which way Missouri would go. By early afternoon almost everybody in town had gathered at the Central Overland station to see the first rider off. However, 4 o'clock came and went, and the train did not arrive with the mail to be sent on to California. William Russell himself was there for the occasion. He was getting some hard looks from his partners, Alexander Majors and William Waddell, who had not been enthusiastic about this expensive venture in the first place. Bolivar Roberts prowled the platform like a bear with a toothache, peering repeatedly down the tracks for any sign of the engine's smoke.

One of the calmest people on the scene was the tough little rider, Billy Richardson. Tuned to a fine pitch for his history-making ride, Billy kept apart from the noisy crowd and said soothing things to his long-legged mare to keep her from getting fidgety from the waiting.

Five o'clock came, and still there was no sign of the train from the east. The crowd began to grumble. A brass band assembled for the occasion played *Hail, Columbia, Dixie,* and *Camptown Races,* then played them again, that being their entire repertoire.

By six the crowd was getting out of hand as the whiskey flowed freely. Russell, Majors, and Waddell were locked in the office arguing about how they were going to salvage the schedule. Bolivar Roberts was hollering at anybody who came near him, and even cool Billy Richardson was getting nervous.

Finally, at six-thirty, a full two and a half hours late, the far-off whistle was heard. Amid drunken cheers from the townspeople, the train chugged into St. Joe. The band, being well into the whiskey, struck up their three pieces simultaneously. Nobody noticed. The local politicians sadly gave up on delivering their send-off speeches and Billy Richardson swung gratefully into the saddle.

Before the train had ground to a full stop, railroad employees hustled the packets of special pony mail across the platform. The letters were written on tissue paper to keep the weight down, and sealed in oiled silk to protect them against rain and sweat on the trip west.

The packets of mail were locked into four pouches on the mochila. Billy Richardson gave a final wave to the cheering crowd and galloped off. The Pony Express was underway.

After horse and rider were ferried across the Missouri River, Richardson settled the mare into a steady ground-eating lope that would most efficiently cover the miles he had to go. He rode through the Kickapoo reservation accompanied by several young sports from St. Joe. The escort dropped away singly and in pairs until before long Billy Richardson was riding alone. He concentrated on making up what he could of the time that had been lost before he started. The twenty miles to the first relay station was covered in a little more than an hour. The two minutes allowed for a switch of horses was cut to one minute and ten seconds as the station keeper flopped the mochila over the saddle of a fresh mount even as Billy climbed aboard.

By the time Richardson turned the mochila over to his relief rider, a youngster named Don Rising, he had made up better than thirty minutes of the lost time.

Rising put the spurs to his horse, and by the time he

finished his run at Hollenburg, another thirty minutes had been saved.

Back in the offices of the Central Overland, Russell, Majors, and Waddell could only hope that things were going well. There would be no news coming back from the Pony route unless some stray eastbound traveler happened to pass a rider on the way. All the three partners could do was wait and worry.

Likewise, wait and worry was all Morgan Bunker could do while sweating it out at Three Fools Creek. The riders heading east, who started from Sacramento the same day Billy Richardson left St. Joe, came through on schedule, but it was the mail heading for California that was crucial. The east-to-west run would make or break the Pony Express.

During his brief changeover at Three Fools, the east bound rider told of heavy late snows in the Sierra Nevadas, but said they should be well melted by the time the west bound rider hit the pass.

"One thing you might keep an eye out for," he added, "there's a suspicious party of Paiutes been seen between here and Stillwater."

"Three braves?" Morgan asked.

The rider nodded. "They been keepin' their distance from the stations, but word is they ain't actin in a natural way for peaceable Injuns."

"If it's the same ones I seen, they were actin' normal enough, if a mite standoffish," Morgan said.

"All I know is what the station hands tell me. I'd be lookin' out for 'em if I was you."

"I will," Morgan said. "Thanks."

The rider climbed aboard his fresh mustang and galloped off to the east as his tired mount was led to the corral by Wilson. Morgan watched the rider until he was out of sight, aching to be in the saddle himself.

On April 10 Morgan went to bed early, but he didn't sleep much. According to the schedule, which he knew by heart, the rider from Camp Floyd was due at six o'clock the next morning. Morgan was up and dressed before the first light, pestering Chops for sourdoughs and coffee. With the first rays of the sun he wandered down to the corral. He had already picked out the mustang he would ride on his first lap—a tough little roan who would run all day if you asked him. Wilson assured him for the fiftieth time that the horse was watered and fed and eager to go.

Back in the station house Morgan checked and rechecked the standard arms that the Pony riders would carry—a pair of Navy Colt revolvers and a Spencer carbine. The firepower seemed a mite excessive to Morgan, since they were under orders to avoid gunplay if at all possible, but those were the rules.

By half-past five he was fully dressed and ready to ride. He stood out on the trail squinting into the rising sun, looking for the rider. It was twenty minutes after six when he saw the dust cloud and heard the horn.

The rider, a feisty Dutchman named Yeager, climbed down breathing hard while Wilson and Garrity swung the mochila to Morgan's horse.

"You're late," Morgan said. "What held you up?"

"Train was late gettin' into St. Joe," said Yeager. "More'n two and a half hours. We've made up better'n half of it so far."

"Any trouble along the way?"

"Kip Davis got chased by some Cheyennes by Medicine Bow, but he outrun 'em easy."

When the mochila was in place, Morgan checked

that the four lock boxes were secure and swung up into the saddle.

"Adios," said Yeager. "Good luck."

Morgan pulled off his slouch hat, gave them all a wave, slapped his mustang on the rump, and rode off to the west.

13

In the chill dawn of April 11, roughly halfway along the route to be ridden by Morgan Bunker, three white men wearing Indian buckskins huddled where a cluster of boulders provided shelter from the cold morning wind. Nearby three Indian ponies grazed along with the horses the men had ridden out from Missouri.

Curly jerked a thumb in the direction of the horses. "Do we have to ride them fool pintos any more? It ain't natural for a white man to straddle a horse with no saddle under him."

"I'll need mine a little longer," Smiler said. "You can turn the other two loose. They've served their purpose."

"I'll be glad when we can shuck these stinkin' Injun duds too," said Pete.

"Amen to that," Curly agreed.

"It won't be long now," Smiler promised. "That Pony rider's due to come through Stillwater Notch before midday. As soon as we've done our business with him we can go pick up our own clothes, burn these Injun skins, and hightail it for California."

"It can't be too soon for me," Curly said.

Pete pointed off toward the hills to the north. "I don't like the looks of that smoke."

The others turned to watch an irregular column of gray smoke rising against the lightening blue sky.

"You reckon the Paiutes are fixin' to come lookin' for them three braves?" Curly said.

"Maybe," Smiler said. "It won't make no difference to us. By the time they find what's left of them redskins, we'll be long gone."

"I surely hope so," said Curly. "I've heard them Paiutes can work on a man all day with a skinnin' knife and keep him alive to watch."

"Let's ride," Smiler said.

They untied the horses, gave two of the Indian ponies a swat on the rump, and watched them gallop off toward the hills.

"It's a damn lucky thing them horses can't talk," Curly said.

"When they get back to the tribe without riders they'll say plenty," Smiler said, "so we better not waste any more time."

The three men headed back toward the Overland Trail, leading Smiler's horse while he rode the third pinto. They drew up at the lip of a rocky cliff overlooking the ravine known as Stillwater Notch. A few feet below where they stood was a narrow ledge from which there would be an excellent shot at anyone riding by on the trail.

Curly and Pete dismounted and let themselves down to the ledge. There they stretched out, getting as comfortable as possible, and trained their rifles on the trail below. Curly twisted his head around to look up at Smiler.

"No way we can miss from here."

Smiler stayed mounted. He pointed off to a hump-backed little hill to the east.

"I'll stand lookout up there. When you boys see me give you the high sign, it means the rider's comin'."

The two men on the ledge grunted that they under-stood. Smiler urged the pony around and headed for the little hill. When he reached the crest he dismounted and sat down to scan the trail, visible from there for a good two miles to the east. In less than an hour he saw something, and stood up for a better look. Shading his eyes against the sun, he saw that it was a lone rider coming at a good clip.

Morgan, his eyes restlessly scanning the horizon, saw the standing figure at the same time. An Indian, from the look of his silhouette and the clean lines of the pony. The distinctive two-feathered headband marked him as a Paiute. The way he was standing alone atop the hill that way meant he was a lookout. The Paiutes Morgan had run across during his learning of the route had given him wide berth, and he did not really expect any trouble this time. Still, there were the stories from the other stations, and he rode on cautiously, keeping his eye on the watching figure.

The Indian turned away from him then and raised an arm in the air. It was clearly a signal to somebody. While maintaining his steady pace, Morgan checked to see that the Colts were free in their holsters. He tried not to be too obvious about it, since there was no real cause to be alarmed. All the same, the lookout on the hill made him uncomfortable.

Then the standing figure mounted and rode down out of Morgan's sight on the other side of the hill. Morgan reined his mustang in sharply. He quickly cal-culated that the last relay station was an hour behind him, erasing any thought of going back. The mail was already late. It had to go through—that was the first and last rule of the Pony Express. Sometimes the procedures had to be altered a little bit to meet the situation.

Morgan guided his horse off the trail and rode around behind the humpbacked hill where he had seen the lookout. No one reappeared on the crest, and Morgan rode in a wide circle, doubling back toward the trail where it cut through Stillwater Notch.

He eased the mustang up to the lip of the cliff and looked over. Below him on the rocky ledge two white men in Indian get-up lay with rifles ready, peering up the trail in the direction he would have come from. Morgan unholstered a revolver. Holding the reins with one hand, he braced the barrel of the colt on his forearm.

"All right, gents," he said, "kindly dump them rifles over the side."

The two men jerked in surprise. Morgan thumbed back the hammer of the Colt, letting the double click give emphasis to his words. The men twisted around to look up at him. The curly-haired one, then the one with the pimples pitched their rifles down to the trail below.

"Now stand up, movin' slow and keepin' your hands where I can see 'em."

The men did as they were told, and turned around to face him.

"Ain't you boys a mite old to be playin' Injun?"

The two men glared at him, saying nothing.

"If you figure on foolin' anybody, you ought to study up some on the way Injuns do things. They mount from the right side of the horse, not the left, the way one of you boys just did up there on the hill."

The men looked at each other quickly, then stared down at their feet.

"Now you just unbuckle them gunbelts," Morgan said, "and toss them over the edge after the rifles."

The curly-haired man followed orders. The other one started to, then made a grab for his pistol.

Morgan fired. The slug caught the man high on the inside of the leg, just below his crotch. He dropped the pistol and went to his knees, his face suddenly gray as blood pumped out over the buckskin pants.

"That was plain dumb," Morgan said. He swung the barrel of the Colt over to cover the curly-haired man, who was staring down at his bleeding companion.

Without warning something punched Morgan painfully in the left side. The ringing crack of a rifle followed immediately, and Morgan knew he'd been shot. The mustang danced around nervously and Morgan caught sight of the lookout in Indian dress aiming a rifle at him from back up the hill.

"Damn," he muttered, cursing his own stupidity.

A boulder chipped at the mustang's feet, and the rifle cracked again. From the corner of his eye Morgan saw the curly-haired man going for the pistol dropped by his companion. To stand and fight it out now, he saw, would just compound his foolishness.

Wincing at the pain in his side, Morgan spurred his horse on along the lip of the bluff until he came to a spot where the slope down the trail was less steep. Every minute he expected the shattering impact of another rifle bullet, but none came. The tough little horse scrambled and slid down the bank to the trail, then took off in a pounding gallop toward the west.

Turning to look back Morgan could see the rifleman from the hill and the curly-haired man coming after him. However, they dropped back quickly as the grain-fed mustang pulled away. Morgan relaxed in the saddle as much as he could with the numbing pain in his side. His shirt and jacket were wet with blood, but it didn't seem to be flowing much now, so maybe nothing vital was hit. The important thing was to hold together until he got to Carson City and turned over the mochila.

When they realized they were not going to catch the Pony Express rider, Smiler and Curly pulled up.

"Goddamn the luck," Smiler growled. "What wised him up?"

"He saw you climb on the pony from the left side and knowed you weren't no Injun," Curly said.

"Well, what was the matter with you two? You both had rifles."

"He had the drop on us, Smiler. When Pete went for his pistol the boy gunned him easy."

"A rotten shame."

"Think we should go back and see about Pete?"

"It'd be a waste of time," Smiler said. "The way he was bleedin', he's a goner for sure."

"I reckon you're right. Let's go back and get our proper duds and light out."

Smiler scowled off in the direction the Pony rider had escaped. "The Widow McKee ain't gonna like this at all."

"We'll have more to worry about than the widow if we hang around these parts much longer," Curly said.

With some reluctance, Smiler turned the Indian pony around, and they rode back to pick up his other horse. They took a quick look at Pete, who was unconscious now in a pool of blood. His breathing was shallow and irregular.

Smiler shook his head. "Like I figured, he's a goner."

They rode north to the boulder that marked the spot where they had hidden their clothes, and changed gratefully out of the Paiute buckskins. Smiler was already mounted, and Curly had his foot in the stirrup when there was a sizzling sound, followed by a solid *thunk*.

Curly grunted and staggered away from his horse, trying vainly to reach around with both hands to his back. As he stumbled in a circle, Smiler saw the feathered end of a Paiute arrow protruding from between Curly's shoulder blades. Looking off toward the hills, he saw a party of a half-dozen braves riding toward them.

"Oh, shit," he muttered, and put the spurs to his horse.

Behind him, Curly sank to his knees, coughing blood. He held out a hand toward the departing Smiler as the Paiutes surrounded him.

White-hot pain lanced through Morgan's side with every jolt of the horse's hooves, and it took all his concentration to stay in the saddle. He would not slow down, because he had lost ten minutes in his skirmish with the ambushers, and he did not want to lose any more time.

As he approached the Pony station at Carson City his vision was impaired by shapeless black spots that seemed to dance in the air between him and whatever he was looking at. When he pulled up in front of the station he sagged in the saddle, feeling he could not have ridden another ten yards. He nearly toppled to the ground before the station keeper caught him.

"What happened to you, son? You're bleedin'."

"Bushwhackers," Morgan got out. "Dressed like Injuns back up the trail by Stillwater Notch."

A couple of station hands swung the mochila across to a fresh horse, and the relief rider climbed aboard. He looked curiously down at the wounded Morgan.

"You gonna be all right?"

Morgan waved him on. "I'm fine. You just start raisin' dust, I cost you ten minutes."

When the rider was away, Morgan walked into the station, leaning gratefully on the keeper. All his strength seemed to have drained away the minute he brought his pony to a stop.

Inside he sat on one of the cots sweating while the keeper peeled away his bloody jacket and shirt. There was a raw red furrow across his ribcage with an angry bruise all around it. The keeper sponged off the wound while Morgan ground his teeth and tried to keep from passing out.

"It looks like the rifle ball just scraped across your rib bones," said the keeper. "That would make you a pretty lucky young man. Providing there ain't no infection."

When the wound was as clean as he could get it, the station keeper drenched it with witch hazel and wrapped a clean white bandage around Morgan's chest.

"Hurt much?" he asked.

"You're darn right it hurts," Morgan said.

"I ain't surprised. Care for a slug o' whiskey to deaden it somewhat?"

"Ain't that against the rules?"

"Not for medicinal use. And if this ain't a medical case, I never seen one."

"I might just try some of that," Morgan said.

The station keeper poured a generous portion of whiskey into a cup and handed it to him. Morgan took a swallow and felt an almost immediate lessening of the pain.

"Good stuff," he said.

"As long as you don't develop too strong a thirst for it. You drink that down and you oughta sleep till morning. If you can walk by then there's a stage comin' through from Virginia City headin' for Sacramento. Out there they got the doctors to fix you up proper."

Morgan was getting drowsy fast, but something in the station keeper's words bothered him.

"What do you mean *if* I can walk?" he said.

"Don't fret about that, son. If you can't, none of the rest matters none anyway."

14

It was the most exciting day for the young city of Sacramento since the heady time following the discovery of gold at Sutter's Mill. Since early morning a crowd of celebrants had milled around downtown, centering their attention on the Central Overland freight office. There a freshly painted sign had been hung reading *Pony Express*. If all had gone well along the two thousand mile route from St. Joseph, the rider carrying the first batch of east-to-west mail would arrive at four o'clock.

Since it was a Friday, the city was prepared to celebrate all weekend. Flags and bunting were everywhere. Bands played, whiskey flowed, politicians made speeches. The mood was carnival.

Things were considerably more subdued in the offices above the stage depot. There all three partners, William Russell, Alexander Majors, and William Waddell were gathered. In contrast to the revelry out in the streets, their mood was tense and worried. The fourth man in the room, Bolivar Roberts, stood gazing stolidly out the window, hands clasped behind his back.

"What time is it?" asked Waddell.

"Half past four," said Majors.

"I knew it," said Waddell. "This was too risky a venture to put all that money into."

"Have a little faith, gentlemen," said Russell. "Even if our man is an hour or two late, even a day, we will still have proved our point. Mail will have been carried across the country faster than anyone dreamed possible. No great stride forward was ever made without a gamble. And the Pony Express was designed with as little gamble involved as possible. Isn't that so, Mr. Roberts?"

The burly superintendent turned from the window to face the partners. "On my trip out here from St. Joseph I personally checked every station along the entire route. They were all shipshape, fully stocked, and ready to go."

"There are so many things that could go wrong," said Waddell, the worrier.

"Everything we can do has been done to see that they go right," Roberts said.

"Has there been any word from Washington?" asked Majors.

"Not yet," Russell admitted.

"Why not? Senator Glin promised he would introduce a bill to get us the mail contract."

"He's holding off until we've proved we can do it. After that, there will be no way they can withhold the contract. Then, gentlemen, the Central Overland Express Company can write its own ticket."

"I'll believe it when I see it," said Waddell.

"Amen," added Majors.

Boliver Roberts turned back to resume his watch out the window to the east.

Two blocks away from the Central Overland office, in one of the best rooms of the Carmichael Hotel, Jessie McKee was in high spirits. She filled two glasses with champagne and lifted her own in a toast.

"They're almost an hour overdue now," she said happily. "I'll bet Old Man Russell is sweating bullets. Drink up, Joe, this is a celebration."

Cherokee Joe tasted his glass of champagne and made a sour face. "What do you want to drink this fizz water for, Jessie? There's good liquor flowin' free as milk all over town."

"That fizz water comes all the way from France, and it costs plenty, so try to enjoy it."

Joe took a swallow and belched. "It don't have much of a kick to it."

"It won't hurt you to stay halfway sober for one day," Jessie said. She turned to young Jack Bunker, who was sitting uncomfortably on a straight-backed chair near the door. "How about you, Jack? You care for a glass of bubbly?"

"No, thank you, ma'am. Alcohol and me ain't such good friends."

"That's not a bad way to keep it," Jessie said, tossing off what remained in her glass and refilling it.

The door opened and Beth Catlin came into the room. "Oh, Mama, there's so much excitement downstairs."

"I can hear it," Jessie said.

"Can't I go down to the depot and watch the Pony rider come in?"

Cherokee Joe snickered. "You'd likely have a good long wait."

Jessie silenced him with a look. She said, "Out on the streets is no place for a young lady to be today with all those drunken miners about. You remember the trouble you had that day in St. Joe."

Jack Bunker spoke up. "Ma'am, I'd be proud to escort Miss Beth down to the stage depot."

Jessie turned and looked him over critically. "Well, I don't know . . ."

"I'd make sure that nobody got out of line," Jack said.

"Please, Mama," Beth coaxed. "I know I'll be all right with Jack along."

"Oh, I suppose if you got it into your head that you gotta go down there, you might as well. But don't stay too long now, hear?"

"I won't, Mama. I just want to look around a little and see if we can catch a glimpse of the rider."

"That's right, ma'am," Jack added. "And after, I'll bring her straight back here."

"You darn well better," Jessie warned.

The two young people went out flushed with excitement. Jessie settled onto the couch with a sigh. Cherokee Joe came over and sat next to her. He put a hand on her leg just above the knee and squeezed it through the velveteen skirt.

"Cut it out," Jessie said. "We don't have time for that stuff now."

"The hell we don't. Them kids'll be gone for an hour at the least. That's time enough to rip off a good one." He shoved his hand up to where her legs joined and massaged her there.

Jessie was breathing faster. "Honest to God, I don't know why I put up with a sidewinder like you."

"Sure you do," Joe said, grinning. "You like to fuck, and I'm the only man you found who knows how to do it right."

"Joe Bunker, you're a mean, dirty, drunken sonofabitch." Jessie leaned back on the couch and spread her legs apart. "But you do have a way about you."

Beth Catlin and Jack came out of the hotel to join the people milling happily about on the street. Beth's eyes were alive and dancing.

"I guess this must be even more exciting than the day in St. Joe when the first rider left heading west," she said.

Young Jack had eyes only for the girl. He said; "How come you and your ma didn't stay around St. Joe for that occasion?"

"Mama said she wanted to be out here for the finish so she could personally laugh at Mr. Russell. She doesn't think the Pony Express is going to make it. But that could be professional jealousy."

"What do you think about the Pony's chances?" Jack asked.

"I don't really know. I try not to get involved with Mama's business dealings."

"That's prob'ly a good idea," Jack said.

"What's your opinion?" Beth lowered her eyes for a moment, then looked up at him. "You have a brother riding for the Pony, don't you?"

"That's right. Not wishin' your ma any bad luck, but if all the riders has the gravel in their gizzard that Morgan has, the Pony Express will make it all right."

Beth blushed, making her look all the prettier.

Jack licked his lips, which had unaccountably gone dry. "Uh, there's a shindig of some sort planned for tonight down at the State Street meetin' house. I don't suppose you'd care to go with me? I mean, if we was properly chaperoned and all?"

Beth gave him a melting sad smile. "That's awfully sweet of you, Jack, but I don't think I should."

"You're bespoken?" he asked quickly.

"Not exactly," she said shyly. "But, well, there is someone."

"Back east?"

"No. I met him in St. Joseph just a month ago. We didn't make any promises or anything, but somehow he's kind of special."

"He's a lucky feller," Jack said, then was immediately embarrassed. He looked eagerly around for something else to talk about. "Say, there seems to be a commotion down in front of the depot."

Beth raised on tiptoe trying to see over the heads of the crowd. "Oh, let's go see what's happening."

The commotion was caused when a local youth who had ridden out toward Placerville to watch for the approach of the Pony rider came galloping down J Street toward the crowd waving his hat and shouting.

"*He's a-comin!*" the young man called, almost falling off his horse in his excitement.

"*He's a-comin'!*" the crowd took up the cry.

In the offices of the Central Overland, Bolivar Roberts heard the cheers below and turned to the three partners wearing his first smile of the day.

"*He's coming in,*" said Roberts.

"What did I tell you?" said Russell.

"Well, that's good news," admitted Majors.

"I'll wait till we hear something from Washington," said Waddell.

Bolivar Roberts excused himself and went downstairs so he could be out in front of the depot when the rider came in. He had always felt more at ease with the riders than with the owners, and that was where he wanted to be for the celebration.

Chosen to bring the mail the final fifty miles from Placerville was a freckle-faced boy of 18 named Trowbridge. He had the look of a 12-year-old, but he was tough as rawhide and looked to be as fresh at the end of his ride as he had been starting out.

As he drew near the stage depot the crowd around the rider made it difficult for him to maneuver his horse through to the front of the building where the reception party waited. When he finally got through, he jumped down and personally removed the mochila with the four lock-boxes of mail and handed it over to Bolivar Roberts. Only then did he turn to wave an acknowledgment to the cheering crowd.

Later, Trowbridge sat in the upstairs office with Roberts and the three partners of the Central Overland to pass along the news he had picked up from the cross-country run.

"Most of the way it was a buggy ride," he said. "No big trouble anyplace, except the other side of Carson City. Our rider got hisself shot up a little by redskins there, only he says they wasn't redskins."

"Morgan Bunker?" Roberts asked quickly.

"That's the feller."

"I knew there'd be trouble," said Waddell.

"How bad was he hit?" Roberts asked.

"I can't rightly say. Leastways, he was healthy enough at the end of his run to pass on the mochila. Word I got was that they'd be bringin' him here to Sacramento by stage. He ought to be here in a couple of days. If he's still alive."

"I don't understand," said Majors. "Were they Indians who shot our man or weren't they?"

"From what I hear they was dressed up like Injuns, but our rider says they was white men."

"This Morgan Bunker was your choice to ride that section, wasn't he, Roberts?" asked Russell.

"Yes, sir, he was. And if Morgan says it was white

men attacked him, I'll guarantee you it was white men."

"I suppose we'll get the full story when he's brought in," said Majors.

"If he doesn't die on the way," said Waddell.

Boliver Roberts spoke to young Trowbridge. "That's all we need for now, son. Why don't you get yourself cleaned up, then go on out and let the folks give you a proper welcome to Sacramento."

The young rider grinned his thanks to Roberts, nodded to the three partners, and left the office. While the others fell into a discussion of costs and revenues, Roberts went back to the window to look out at the celebrating crowd. His personal celebration would wait until he knew the condition of Morgan Bunker.

Down in the street Beth Catlin clapped her hands and laughed, carried away by the excitement of the crowd. Jack Bunker stayed close to her side, watching her the way a puppy watches his mistress. Her blue eyes sparkled, her cheeks were flushed with her enjoyment of the moment.

All around them couples were hugging and kissing, using the celebration as an excuse for public affection. Jack Bunker ached to hold this lovely girl in his arms and share the excitement with her. He would too, Jack told himself, it if weren't for some faceless man back in St. Joe who had found her first. Maybe Jack Bunker had not always played according to the rules, but he was not one to jump another man's claim. Maybe if he and this other Jasper could meet face-to-face . . . but that was for thinking about another time.

"Maybe we'd better head back to your hotel," he said. "Your ma might be wonderin' after you."

"Oh, I don't think so," Beth said. "Let's just walk

around a little and enjoy the noise. That is, if you don't mind."

"I don't mind a bit," Jack said quickly.

"Anyway," Beth said, linking her arm through his in a sisterly way, "I think Mama had some business she wanted to take care of with your father."

They walked on among the celebrants, together, but with an invisible wall between them. For Jack it was like being near starved and tied up just out of reach of a banquet.

Jessie McKee raised her head to look over the pumping naked buttocks of Cherokee Joe toward the window. "What's all that hollering about outside?"

"Damnit, woman, if you'll keep your mind on what you're doin' for another minute, we'll go find out."

Jessie concentrated on what she was doing, and in even less than a minute Cherokee Joe rolled off of her with a satisfied groan. Jessie pulled the comforter from the bed and wrapped it around herself. Leaving Joe sprawled where he was, she crossed to the window and looked out.

"Sonofabitch!"

Joe raised his head. "What's the matter?"

"That goddamn Pony Express Rider must have made it after all. I can see that Bolivar Roberts grinning all the way from here."

"There was always a chance they'd get through, wasn't there?"

Jessie turned away from the window and the cheering crowd below. In a voice too low for Joe to hear she muttered, "There wouldn't have been if Smiler had done the job he was sent to do."

the week that followed young Trowbridge's triumphant arrival.

Late one night a lone rider entered the city who had no thoughts of celebrating. Smiler Tate was tired and dirty and worried about what the future held for him. He left his horse at a livery stable and made directly for the hotel room of Jessie McKee.

Jessie was less than overjoyed to see him. She locked the door to make sure they would not be interrupted, and faced him with eyes of cold fire.

"There are two things I want to know from you," she said, her voice dangerously soft. "First, why did you pick Cherokee Joe Bunker's son to bushwhack?"

"I had no way of knowin' who'd be ridin' that stretch of the trail," Smiler pleaded. "I just picked me the best place I could find to set up an ambush."

"We'll let that go for now," Jessie said. "The second thing I want to know is how come three grown men waiting in ambush couldn't get the best of a boy riding alone."

"Blamed if I know," Smiler said. "Somehow the kid figgered out what we was up to and snuck around to get the drop on Curly and Pete. They never had a chance."

"And what the hell were you doing while this kid was sticking up your partners?"

"I was up on a hill standin' lookout and never had time to get back there. I did get off one shot and winged the kid, I think, but I was mounted and couldn't steady the horse to take aim for a second shot."

Jessie gave a snort of disgust and turned away from him.

"I tried to give chase," Smiler said, "but I was ridin'

a danged Injun pony and couldn't keep up with the boy's mustang."

"And where are your brave compadres now?"

"The kid gunned Pete. Curly took a Paiute arrow. I just barely got out with my skin whole."

"Some people have all the luck," Jessie grumbled. She made an effort to compose herself. "All right, we missed that chance, let's hope we get another. It's a good thing my people in Washington are better at their jobs than you are at yours. At least they're keeping the mail contract tied up for now, but that won't last if the Pony Express keeps delivering the way it started out. If we get another shot at them, we'd better not miss."

"What do you want me to do now, Jessie?" Smiler asked.

"If I was you, I'd get myself out of sight for a while. Cherokee Joe is walking around here all red-eyed about his boy being bushwhacked."

"He don't know we're the ones did it, does he?"

"He's got some ugly suspicions. He don't like you much anyway, so maybe you better be scarce for a while."

"I ain't afraid of that rummy."

"Don't sell Cherokee Joe short. He may have a fondness for the bottle, but when he gets riled he can be a dangerous man. I've got enough to worry about without two of my own men locking horns. You get yourself down to Frisco for a couple of days. I'll let you know when I need you."

Smiler hesitated for a moment, as though he would say something more, then changed his mind and left the room. As he walked out of the hotel downstairs a voice from the darkness brought him up short.

"Hold it, Smiler."

He turned slowly in the direction of the voice. Cherokee Joe emerged from the shadows into the pool of light that spilled through the plate glass window from the lobby.

"Appears you been doin' some travelin'," Bunker said.

"Maybe."

"Been in Utah Territory, have you?"

"I rode through," Smiler said carefully.

"Have any trouble?"

"Lost a couple of my men to the Paiutes."

"That's a shame. I don't suppose you crossed paths with the Pony Express rider."

"Nope. If he went past us, it must of been at night."

"I guess you heard my boy took a rifle ball the other side of Carson City."

"The widow just told me about it. Too bad."

"Some sonofabitch back-shot him. If I ever find out who did it, I'm gonna kill him." Cherokee Joe's voice betrayed no emotion, but his eyes burned dangerously.

"Best you see to it he don't get you first," Smiler said.

"I aim to be careful about who I turn my back on," Joe said.

The two men faced each other grimly for a long moment, then turned and walked their separate ways.

16

THE stage carrying Morgan Bunker arrived in Sacramento the same day Smiler Tate lit out for San Francisco. Morgan's wound had not healed as well as was hoped, and it had been a painful journey from Carson City for him. When they pulled up to the depot he was running a high fever and was too weak to stand without help. Bolivar Roberts wrapped one powerful arm around him and half-carried him to the buggy he had waiting.

The Central Overland paid the bill to put Morgan up in a private room at one of the city's cleaner hotels. The hotel had a doctor in residence, and the company hired a nurse to attend their wounded rider full-time.

Once Morgan was bedded down as comfortably as possible the doctor took Bolivar Roberts out into the hall for a consultation.

"The damage done by the bullet is only superficial," the doctor said. "It was deflected by the ribs and prevented from doing any serious harm. There's some torn muscle tissue, but that should heal quickly. The real problem, as we usually find with bullet wounds, is infection. There was an adequate bandage put on at the time, but it's hard to do a proper job without sterile conditions."

"How bad is it, Doc?" Roberts asked.

"I can't give you a definite answer on that. All we can do for now is keep him quiet, keep the wound drained, and wait. The next few days will tell the story."

The first visitor who came to see Morgan was his father. Cherokee Joe was sober for the occasion, his beard and moustache neatly trimmed. He wore his good suit. The nurse hovered around Morgan's bed at first, but after Joe turned his road agent glare on her she decided there was business to attend to elsewhere.

"Well . . . howdy, son," Joe began, trying to sound natural.

"Pa."

"How you feelin'?"

"A mite puny, but all things considered, it could be a heap worse."

"I reckon."

There was a long pause in the conversation. Cherokee Joe strolled around the room, taking an exaggerated interest in the furnishings.

"Nice room."

"Nice enough."

"Must cost pretty dear."

"I wouldn't know. The Central Overland's payin' the bill."

"Well, they sure ought to. From what I hear, you did yourself proud out there on the trail."

"Got myself shot is what I did."

"But you brought the mail through."

"That's my job."

Joe pulled out a cheroot and started to strike a

match, then he stopped and looked awkwardly at his son. "This won't bother you none, will it?"

Morgan gave him a weak grin. " 'Course not, Pa."

Cherokee Joe lit up, being careful to fan the smoke away from the bed.

"Tell me, son, you got any idea who them snakes were that ambushed you?"

"Never seen 'em before. Leastwise, not the two I got a look at. The other one stayed at a distance. If I'd had my wits about me I shoulda knowed the lookout would be back behind me somewhere."

"They tell me you gunned one of 'em."

"Had to. The damn fool went for his iron while I had him covered."

"It seems queer that ordinary outlaws would go to all the fuss of dressin' up like Injuns."

"I can't figure it," Morgan said.

The nurse came back in and wrinkled her nose at Cherokee Joe's stogie. She marched across the room and threw open the window.

Taking the hint, Joe ground out the cigar against the sole of his boot and dropped the butt into a pocket.

"Uh, is there anything you're needin', son?"

"No, thanks, Pa. They're takin' good care of me here. The doc says I just gotta stay on my back and keep quiet until the fever runs its course and I start gettin' my strength back."

"Well, if there's anything I can do, you just send word."

"I will."

"Reckon I'll be on my way then."

"So long, Pa. Thanks for comin' up."

Cherokee Joe exchanged a final glare with the nurse and went out.

It was frustrating to Morgan that a little old scrape

across the ribs could keep him in bed like this. Although he didn't get any sicker in the next few days, he didn't get any better either. The nights were the worst. Sometimes he would wake up soaked in his own sweat. He had the same fever dream over and over. He was back on the ridge over Stillwater Notch where he shot one of the bushwhackers. Then he would whirl toward the rifleman up on the hill, but he could never get off the second shot.

During the day he felt a little better, but still weak as a baby. Mostly he just lay there staring at the ceiling and trying to will the strength back into his body. Twice a day the doctor came in to lance the wound and drain off the pus and bad blood. Bolivar Roberts visited him often bringing news of the continuing success of the Pony Express.

It was a week exactly from the day he'd been brought in that Morgan awoke and knew for a certainty that he was getting better. His sleep had been dreamless, and the fever was way down. He could still barely sit up without help, but he fancied he could already feel himself getting stronger.

That was the day Beth Catlin came to visit, along with his brother Jack.

"I'd have come sooner," Beth said, "but Mama had me stuck down in San Francisco."

"Well, I'm right glad you made it," Morgan said. "You too, Jack."

"I didn't know till today that you two was acquainted," Jack said.

"We met back in St. Joe," Morgan said.

"That so?" Jack looked quickly at Beth, then back at his brother. "I guess you two'll have things to talk about, so maybe I'll take a walk for myself."

"Don't run off, Jack," Morgan said, but the words lacked conviction.

"I'll be back in a little bit," Jack said, and went out of the room.

When they were alone Beth came over and sat in the chair close to the head of the bed.

"I'm truly sorry to see you feeling so poorly," she said. "Does it hurt very much?"

"Naw. It's just the blame sweatin' I do that drains the strength."

Beth laid a soft, cool hand on his brow. "You do have a temperature. I wish I could do something to help."

"You already perked me up a good deal just by bein' here."

"What a sweet thing to say."

She took his hand and held it while they talked about the way the weather was warming up and how Beth liked San Francisco and whether Morgan was getting enough to eat. The things they said to each other with their eyes were considerably more personal. When Jack returned they both blushed as though they had been caught at some mischief.

"I'd better go now," Beth said. "Mama doesn't know I came to see you. I don't think she'd be happy about it if she found out."

"We did get off to an embarrassin' start," Morgan said.

She leaned over and brushed her lips across his cheek. "If I get a chance I'll come back."

Morgan could still feel the touch of her lips as she went out the door, giving him a little smile over her shoulder. He reached down under the blanket and touched himself. Shoot, he thought, if a man can get all hot and bothered like this by a female, he can't be so all-fired sick.

17

MORGAN did not sleep much the night after his visit from Beth Catlin. It was not, however, the discomfort of his wound that kept him awake. Nor was it dreams of the shooting at Stillwater Notch. The dreams that disturbed his sleep were of the blonde girl and the cool touch of her lips, and other things that made him blush to think about in the daytime.

That evening he had just finished a dinner of pallid stew when the nurse looked in.

"You have a visitor," she said, with a peculiar smirk. "A *lady* visitor."

Morgan's heart leaped at the thought that Beth had returned. "Well, send her on in."

But it was not Beth Catlin who came into the room, it was the Widow McKee. She looked different than Morgan had ever seen her. Her hair was down around her shoulders, all soft and shiny, and she smelled better than a flower garden in a summer breeze.

"Hello, Morgan." She came over and lifted the tray of dinner dishes off his bed.

"Howdy, Miz McKee. You don't have to fuss with them dishes. The nurse'll do that."

Jessie carried the tray over and put it down on a table near the window. While she was there she lowered the window blind, cutting off the setting sun and leaving the room in a rosy dusk.

"I told the nurse to take herself a rest," she said. "I think I can take care of anything that needs doing for you while I'm here."

Morgan swallowed hard. "That's mighty kind of you, Miz McKee."

"Not at all. I like doing for a man, and I don't get much chance these days." She came back and sat down beside the bed. The fresh flowery perfume made Morgan a little dizzy.

"Are the Central Overland people taking good care of you?" she said.

"Oh, yes, ma'am. They're payin' for this room and all the doctorin'. They're even keepin' my regular salary comin', even though I ain't in condition to do any ridin' yet."

"If you ask me, they owe it to you. After all, you were hurt in the line of duty."

"Yes, ma'am."

Jessie reached over to smooth the sheet flat across Morgan's stomach. A shiver went through him. Somehow it made him feel good and guilty at the same time.

"Who gives you your baths?"

"Ma'am?"

"Who washes you? The nurse?"

"Oh, no, ma'am. I ain't so weak that I can't get up to take my own bath and, uh, other personals."

Jessie laughed. A low, honey-coated laugh. "I don't blame you. Your nurse must be sixty years old, and built like a pork barrel. It wouldn't be too much fun getting bathed by her."

Morgan felt his ears growing hot. "She's a real kindly lady, though," he said.

"I'm sure she is. There are some things, though, that a man likes to have done by a woman who's, well, a little better put together."

She smoothed the sheet again, down lower this time. Morgan flinched.

"What's wrong, dear, does it hurt?"

"No, *ma'am*! Not down there it don't."

Jessie laughed softly. "Well, that's one good thing, isn't it?"

"Uh, yes, ma'am."

The Widow McKee made no move to take her hand away from there. Things happened to Morgan over which he had no control. He blushed.

"My, my," Jessie said, moving her hand gently back and forth. "You *are* healthy enough down in that region, aren't you?"

Morgan groaned a little.

"Do these covers bother you?" she asked. "Let me just peel them back a bit and give your body a chance to breathe."

Morgan remembered suddenly that he was wearing only a miserable short night shirt that the nurse had provided for him. He made a futile grab for the covers as Jessie stripped them away.

"There now, dear, you just rest easy. I'll bet it's been quite a long time since you've really been with a woman."

Morgan felt mighty strange lying there naked from the waist down with a good-looking woman sitting right there looking at him. Nothing like this had ever happened to him, and he was amazed at how it fired him up.

"It has been quite a while, I guess." He tried in vain to match Jessie's calm tone.

While she looked into his eyes, Jessie's fingers were doing things to him down below that made him want to cry out in pleasure. A part of his mind reminded him that this woman was old enough to be his mother, but right then he didn't give a hoot.

"I guess the people at Central Overland must think an awful lot of you," she said.

"I, uh, hope so." Morgan tried hard to concentrate on what she was saying, not on what she was doing with her fingers.

"A young man who came through the way you did under fire, well, I'll bet they'll trust you with about anything from now on."

"I don't know about that."

"Oh, I'll bet they will." With her free hand Jessie lightly touched the bandage over his wounded ribs. "Does this hurt much?"

"Right now it don't hurt at all."

She smiled at him. The fiery green eyes seemed to eat him up.

"Do you remember I once offered you a job with Ace Freighters?"

"Yes, ma'am."

"The offer is still good. Except now it's for the job of line supervisor."

"That's kind of you, ma'am, but I ain't experienced along that line."

"I'm sure you could handle the job."

"I'm happy with the job I got."

"Whatever Bill Russell is paying you, I'll double it."

"Double?"

Jessie took her hand away, and Morgan had a sudden feeling of abandonment.

Her voice got lower and more whispery. "Morgan, do you want me to make you feel good?"

"Feel good?"

"The way a woman does for a man." She looked down at him. "From the looks of you, you're more than ready for it."

"To tell you the truth, ma'am, I'd like that a whole lot. But even though I can get in and out of bed pretty good, I ain't so hot at movin' around yet."

"Don't worry about that," she told him. "You just lay right where you are. Stay relaxed and let me do the moving."

Morgan's eyes bugged as Jessie stood up and took her clothes off right there in front of him. Even the Pryor sisters, who were about as randy as any females he ever heard of, always made him turn his back when they stripped down. Jessie McKee moved with a gracefulness that made him ache from wanting her. When she was naked she stood over him close to the bed.

"Put your hand here, Morgan."

"There?"

Jessie took hold of his shaking hand and guided it up between her legs to the area she had indicated. He marveled at the silkiness of her hair down there. The Pryor sisters' was all crisp and curly. Jessie's lower hair was a rich auburn, a shade darker than that on her head.

"Does that feel good?" she asked.

Morgan mumbled something that meant yes. His fingers seemed to take on a life of their own as Jessie pressed his hand against her. He could feel her grow moist and slippery.

"There is a way you could keep your job with Russell and draw a salary from my outfit too," she said.

"Excuse me?"

Jessie climbed onto the bed, moving carefully so as not to jostle him. She positioned herself kneeling above him, her knees planted on either side of his hips.

She ran her fingers lightly over his cheek. "You could be very useful to me just by passing on little bits of information you might pick up about the plans the Central Overland is making."

"That'd be like spyin', wouldn't it?"

Ever so gently Jessie lowered herself onto his erect penis. When she touched him down there he thought he would explode.

"Yes, I suppose you could call it spying," she said. "But these days, with the competition so tough, we've all got to do it to stay in business."

Morgan stared down his body, watching Jessie take him inside her slowly, slowly, a little at a time. He forced his eyes away and looked at the full swaying breasts, the smiling mouth, the glowing green eyes.

"I don't think I could do that, Miz McKee."

Jessie lowered herself suddenly the rest of the way, taking the full length of him into her. Although she seemed not to be moving, all manner of things were happening to Morgan down there.

"I hope you'll think about my offer," she said. "I can be very generous."

Morgan tried to answer, but his breath was coming too rapidly for him to form the words. He forgot all about talking as the red-haired woman began to raise and lower her body, impaled on him all the while. Faster and faster she rode him, her buttocks slapping wetly against his pelvis on the downstroke.

Morgan let go in a burst of pleasure that filled the

whole room with twinkly stars. His breath came out in a long sigh that was halfway a laugh. Jessie smiled down at him, her teeth very white in the red mouth. Suddenly her expression changed to one of surprise. She bounced up and down in a new, urgent rhythm, finally subsiding with a little whimpering cry.

Afterward, she took the basin off the chest of drawers and sponged him off tenderly, but not so tenderly that he didn't start getting hard down there again. She splashed him playfully with cold water and put a stop to that.

"I don't want to use up all your energy in just one day," she said.

Morgan lay relaxed and grinning while she toweled him dry and covered him up again. She stood back then and put on her clothes while he watched. This time he felt no embarrassment.

"You will think about that job with Ace Freighters, won't you?" she said.

"I'm sorry, Miz McKee, I just couldn't do it. As long as I'm on the Central Overland's payroll I figure they deserve all my time."

The green eyes flashed in anger for a moment, then Jessie relaxed into a smile.

"I guess the truth is I would have thought less of you if you'd taken me up on it."

"I'm glad you feel that way about it," Morgan said.

Jessie smoothed the dress down over her stomach and thighs. She smiled. "And the evening certainly wasn't a total loss. There is one thing you can still do for me, though."

"Ma'am?"

"Start calling me Jessie."

18

IT was impossible to say how much the visit from the Widow McKee had to do with it, but Morgan began to recover almost from the moment she left his bed. The stubborn infection in his bullet wound cleared up, the chills and fever disappeared, and his strength began rapidly to return. The doctor attributed his recovery to the efficacy of the medical treatments, but the nurse began giving the young man knowing looks.

Jessie did not come back after the one visit, nor did Beth Catlin return. Morgan was disappointed, but at the same time relieved. He was not really comfortable about his intimacy with the older woman, and he would not have known how to act around Beth so soon after getting acquainted with her mother.

Still, he was curious, and when his brother Jack stopped by, Morgan was quick to steer the conversation.

"I, uh, don't suppose you've seen anything of Beth Catlin?"

"The Widow McKee sent her back down to stay with some folks she knows in San Francisco," Jack said. "It seems she don't think Sacramento is refined enough for her daughter."

"Miz McKee just might be more worried than she needs to be about that gal," Morgan said.

"You could be right." Jack looked embarrassed. "Uh, tell me, Morgan, would you by any chance be sweet on Beth Catlin?"

"Well, now, things hasn't progressed as far as all that, but I do admit that I sort of enjoy havin' her around." Morgan looked closely at his brother. "Why, Jack? Is there anything goin' on between you two?"

"No, I swear it," Jack said quickly. "I did squire the gal around some while she was here, but that was only as a favor to the widow."

"Hey, take it easy," Morgan said. "I'm not accusin' you of anything."

Jack stared down at his boots for a moment, then looked up to meet his brother's gaze. "Truth to tell, I did have me some notions about her. She's a mighty pretty gal. Well-spoken and mannerly too."

"That she is," Morgan agreed. "And I surely can't blame you for noticin' the fact."

"But I never did or said anything romantical," Jack insisted. "Not that I didn't think about it."

"A man can't always be accountable for his thoughts."

"Anyhow, I had a notion you might be sweet on her, and I wasn't goin' to take up with her as long as you were laid up in bed."

"I appreciate that, brother," Morgan said, "but I'm feelin' sprightly enough to get out of this bed right now, and as far as you and me and Beth Catlin is concerned, it's every man for himself."

"You mean that? You ain't mad at me?"

"I ain't heard you say anything I ought to be mad about."

"Fair enough. As soon as you're up and around, I might just give you a run for that little gal."

"May the best man win," Morgan said.

The two brothers grinned at each other for a moment in honest affection, then Jack turned away embarrassed.

"Reckon I better get a move on. The widow's got some work for me up the line in Yuba City."

"So long, Jack. Take care of yourself."

"You too, Morgan."

On his way out of Morgan's room, Jack almost ran into Bolivar Roberts coming in. The Central Overland superintendant marched to the foot of Morgan's bed and took a stance there with his hands planted on his hips.

"Your lollygaggin' days are over, son. The doctor says you're fit enough to be up and around."

"Well, hot dog!" Morgan threw back the covers and swung his feet to the floor. "I coulda told him that days ago."

"You feel ready to go back to work?"

"Do I!" Morgan exclaimed. "Just put me back on a pony and I'll show you."

"You'll be back on the run soon enough," Roberts said, "but what I have in mind for you now is more in the nature of a special assignment."

"Oh?" Morgan stood up, felt momentarily dizzy, and sat back down on the bed.

"Don't try to rush things," Roberts told him. "I want you to take a couple of days to get your legs back under you so you'll be ready to travel."

"Travel where?"

"You know Julesburg?"

"I do."

"We're having some problems with the station there. It seems they're a mite slipshod in their procedures for sending the mail through."

"Slipshod?"

"I've got reports that the food and beds for our riders are not up to the company standards. Worst of all, the horses are not being properly cared for."

"What's goin' on there, anyhow?"

"It looks like the Central Overland made a big mistake in the man they put in charge."

"Jules Reni?"

"You've heard of him?"

"Most everybody has."

"I suppose so. He's run the show in that territory for a long time, and the company thought that by putting him in charge they were taking out insurance. It hasn't worked out that way."

"Where do I fit in?" Morgan asked.

"I'm getting to that. As you probably know, this Jules Reni carries a reputation as a dangerous man to fool around with. He's dug in so deep in Julesburg, that it won't be an easy job rooting him out. In fact, it's no job at all for a man without experience in that line of work. Now it so happens that the Central Overland does have one man on the payroll who might be able to handle Reni. I put it to him, and he agreed."

"It's a big job for one man," Morgan said.

"That's what I figured. Especially since there's nobody in Julesburg we can really trust, what with Reni doing the hiring there. I asked our man how many of our people he thought he'd need. He said just one. And he asked for you."

"Me?" Morgan was dumbfounded. "Who is this feller, anyhow?"

Roberts flipped open the case of his watch. "I asked him to come up here today. He ought to be along any minute now."

The words were barely spoken when the door opened and the nurse looked in.

"A gentleman outside," she said.

"We're expecting him," Roberts said.

The nurse stepped out of the way and Jack Slade entered. His wide shoulders nearly brushed the sides of the doorway. Slade was dressed as he had been the first time Morgan met him in St. Joseph, in black frock coat and planter's hat, which he now held in one hand. The black moustache was neatly clipped, the bullet eyes hard and unsmiling as ever.

He nodded to Bolivar Roberts, then said, "Hello, Morgan."

"Howdy, Captain Slade."

"I hear you got yourself in the way of a rifle ball."

Morgan grinned self-consciously. "I ran into a little trouble on the trail."

"The way I heard it, you handled yourself right well," said Slade.

"I managed to shoot one of them rascals before they plunked me in the back, but mostly I just outran 'em."

"They found the one you shot," Slade told him. "He died of the wound. Another one wasn't so lucky. The Paiutes put an arrow in him, then skinned him alive."

Morgan shook his head. "I bear no love for them bushwhackers, but that's a hard way for any man to go out."

"Most times a man gets what he asks for," said Slade. "I hear there were three of them."

"That's right. There was the two waitin' for me in ambush, and a third standin' lookout. He's the one that shot me."

"Well, it seems one of them is still walking around. Maybe you'll have another chance at him."

Morgan was not sure he wanted another chance, but he said nothing.

"What I'm here for is to ask if you want to ride along with me to help take care of a little company business in Julesburg."

"I'd be more than proud to, Captain Slade."

Slade turned to the superintendent. "Did you explain the situation to him, Mr. Roberts?"

"I told him what's involved."

"As I understand it," Morgan said, "the main idea is to get rid of Jules Reni."

"That's about the size of it," Slade said. "It won't be any picnic."

"I wouldn't expect one," Morgan said.

"I don't know how many men Reni has, but I don't like to clutter myself up with a whole crowd. One good man to cover my back is all I need."

"I hope I can fill the bill," Morgan said.

"You already showed me a quick eye when those highwaymen held up our stage. I know you can ride, or you wouldn't be a part of the Pony Express. And it appears you can handle a six-gun."

"My pa taught me when I was a youngster."

"I plan to leave in four days," Slade said. "Will you be ready to travel?"

"Shoot, I'm ready to travel now," Morgan said. "I don't care what the doctor says."

"Four days will be plenty soon enough," Slade said. "Does that meet with your approval, Mr. Roberts?"

"I've got no objections."

"Fine. I'll see you then, Morgan."

Slade and Bolivar Roberts went out together, leaving Morgan elated over the assignment. He was still in high spirits that evening when Cherokee Joe came to see him. Joe was not looking his best. He needed a shave, his eyes were rheumy, and his hand showed a tremor.

"Well, son," he said with false heartiness, "I hear you'll be up and around soon."

"That's right, Pa. Good as new."

"That's fine. Yessir, I'm right glad to hear that." Joe sat down in the chair next to the bed, nearly losing his balance before he caught himself.

"Pa, you're kinda heavy into the bottle again, ain't you?"

Joe stiffened his back in a try at dignity. "A man needs a little swig now and then."

"Little swig?"

"Well, maybe I'm liftin' the glass a bit more than usual, but why shouldn't I? It's been most a month now I been stuck here in Sacramento. I ain't no city man, you know that. I belong out where a man's got room to fart without fannin' the air."

"What's Miz McKee got you doin'?" Morgan asked.

Joe looked away. "A little of this and a little of that." He glanced sideways back at his son. "I hear she offered you a job."

"I already got a job," Morgan said. He wondered what else the old man had heard about his encounter with the widow.

"It would of been nice," Joe said, "you, me, and Jack all workin' for the same outfit. Together again like it used to be."

Morgan said nothing.

"I hear tell Jack Slade himself was up to see you," Joe said, his eyes turning sly.

"That's so," Morgan said.

"You and him acquainted, are you?"

"Captain Slade works for the Central Overland too. We rode out on the stage from St. Joe together."

"Must of been an interestin' trip."

"It was," Morgan said, wondering where his father was headed.

"He have anything special in mind when he come to see you?"

"He just stopped by to wish me well," Morgan said. "Him and Mr. Roberts." He felt bad about lying to his father, but Cherokee Joe should have known better than to ask him questions about Central Overland business.

The minutes ticked by, and neither father nor son could find anything more to talk about. The silence grew steadily more oppressive.

Finally Cherokee Joe slapped his knees and said, "Well, I guess I'll amble along."

"I'm glad you stopped by, Pa."

"Why, sure. It does me good to see you lookin' so chipper, son. You take care of yourself, hear?"

"I will, Pa."

Cherokee Joe rose awkwardly from the chair and walked out the door, making an obvious effort to keep his gait steady. For some reason he couldn't figure out, Morgan felt tears in his eyes.

19

MORGAN'S recovery was rapid over the next four days. He ate with a vigorous appetite and quickly gained back the weight he had lost during his time in bed. In the mornings he hired a horse and rode through the hills that surrounded Sacramento. He spent the afternoons walking around the city getting the feel of having his legs under him again.

He saw no more of Cherokee Joe nor his brother Jack. Beth Catlin was banished to San Francisco. Once Morgan did meet the widow McKee by chance outside the hotel.

"Hello, Morgan," she said. The knowing smile on her face would have made him blush in the old days, but not any more.

"Howdy, Jessie." He had not forgotten her half-joking request when she left his bedside.

"You're looking fit."

"Near as good as new."

"You haven't changed your mind about the job we talked about?"

"Nope. Sorry."

"That's too bad. But if you feel like talking, about the job offer or anything else, you know where I am."

"I'll keep that in mind."

Actually, Morgan had no intention of ever getting that close to the widow again. Not because he hadn't enjoyed it, certainly. He was afraid that if Jessie McKee ever got those fine long legs properly wrapped around him, he would never get himself untangled. For the first time he understood what kept his father hanging around.

Jessie's eyes told him she understood all this, and a whole lot more. She gave his hand an intimate little squeeze that made him tingle all the way down to his crotch. It was a good thing, he decided, that he was leaving in the morning with Jack Slade, or he might not be strong enough to stay away from this woman.

The stagecoach ride from Sacramento to Julesburg was without undue excitement, although everybody kept a sharp lookout for hostile Indians as they rolled through Paiute country. The other passengers were somewhat awed to be riding with the notorious Jack Slade. The taciturn captain, as usual, kept his thoughts to himself. Morgan marveled that while the rest of them got uncommonly rumpled and grimy over the long trip, Captain Slade somehow managed to stay as fresh looking as he had been the minute he stepped aboard.

It was a bright, crisp morning in the second week of May when the coach finally rattled into Julesburg. A light rain the night before had settled the dust, but had not lasted long enough to turn the streets to mud. The air was fresh and the sun rode high in a blue-white sky. The street was crowded with boisterous citizens.

The passengers climbed down from the stage and

stretched their cramped limbs. Aside from a faint twinge at the ribs when he twisted his body, Morgan felt no discomfort from his recent wound. The furrow made by the bullet was healed over with a pale scar that he was secretly a little proud of. During the trip Captain Slade had made no concessions to him because of the wound, had not, in fact, even mentioned it. For this Morgan was grateful to him. He'd had enough of being treated like an invalid.

The two men stood on the platform of the stage depot and took their bags as the driver handed them down.

"You want me to go get us a room at the hotel, Captain?" Morgan said.

Slade shook his head. "No sense settling in before we know if we're staying. We'll leave the bags here for now. It's best to get started with our business before the whole town knows we're here."

They walked into the station and set the two carpetbags on the counter.

"Mind keeping an eye on these for us?" Slade said.

"Sure thing." The stationmaster swung the two carpetbags down behind the counter. When he straightened up he stared curiously at Slade.

"Do I know you from somewhere, mister?"

"Not likely," Slade answered shortly. He turned and strode out of the station.

Outside Morgan glanced at him curiously.

"In my line of work it's a bad sign when a man's face gets too familiar," Slade said.

They walked up the street to the Central Overland office, which also served as the Pony Express station. Inside four men sat around a makeshift table playing poker. Morgan saw at a glance that they were not Pony riders. Too old and too heavy. Another man sat slumped in a swivel chair behind a desk. His feet were up on the desk and a derby hat was tipped down over his eyes.

Slade came to a stop in the middle of the room and looked around. The card players glanced up briefly at him and Morgan, then returned to their game. The man behind the desk snored softly.

"Anybody working here?" Slade asked in a cold, quiet voice.

The poker game stopped, but none of the players said anything. Slade gave each of them a long look, then walked over to the man who was sleeping at the desk. Morgan took up a position by the door, watching for anybody to make a quick move. The men at the table were careful to keep their hands in sight.

With a sweep of his arm Slade knocked the sleeping man's boots off the desk top. He lurched forward in the chair, his hat falling into his lap.

"What the hell do you think you're doin'?" the man sputtered.

"Do you work here," Slade said in a voice cold as gunmetal, "when you're awake?"

"Yeah. I'm in charge."

"I thought Jules Reni was in charge."

The man looked at Slade more closely. "Well, sure, he's the big boss."

"Then he's the one I want to see."

The man looked over to make sure the four men were still watching. "So you want to see Mr. Reni, do you? And just who the hell might you be?"

"My name is Slade. Captain Jack Slade."

There was a sudden silence in the room, and the color drained out of the face of the man behind the desk. The poker players quickly returned to studying their cards.

The desk man nearly knocked his chair over scrambling to his feet. "Sorry, Mr. Slade, nobody told me you was comin', or I'd of had everything lookin' more ship-shape around here."

"That's *Captain* Slade."

"Oh, right." The man bobbed his head up and down eagerly.

"And I didn't advertize the fact that I was coming."

"Well . . . sure. Why should you?"

"Now where's Reni?"

"Well, uh, he ain't here right now, Mr. I mean Captain Slade."

There was a painful silence that stretched out for several seconds. One of the poker players, a thin, sallow-faced gunman, got up as casually as he could manage and eased past Morgan out the door. Morgan glanced at Slade, who signaled to let him go.

Slade unbuttoned his frock coat, letting the desk man get a look at his holstered revolvers. "I can see that Reni isn't here, friend," he said. "I'm waiting for you to tell me where he is."

"Oh, right. Most prob'ly you'll find him down at the Buckskin Saloon. He's got an office there. It's at the end of the street." He began to perspire.

Slade started for the door, then turned back halfway across the room. "By the way, friend, what's your name?"

"It's Ingram, Captain Slade. Amos Ingram. If there's anything I can do for you while you're in town, anything at all, you just say the word."

"I'll remember that," Slade said. Ingram was sweating heavily when they walked out.

When they were outside Morgan said, "I guess you saw that skinny cuss sneak out the door."

"I saw him."

"You reckon he hightailed it up to tell Jules Reni we're lookin' for him?"

"I wouldn't be surprised. There was no sense trying to stop him, since I'm sure Reni would get the message one way or another."

As they walked up the street toward the Buckskin Saloon and Card Club Morgan sensed a change in the atmosphere of the town. Activity seemed to have been suspended. Men stood in small, closed groups, talking in low voices, throwing covert glances at the two strangers. Here and there a face could be seen peering from behind a window. Women and children had disappeared from the street as though by magic.

"Do you think there's gonna be trouble, Captain?" Morgan asked.

"Sooner or later, but not right away, I would think. Reni will want to know what we're after before he makes a move. But be wary all the same."

They pushed through the batwing doors into the Buckskin. The saloon was unusually crowded for the morning hour, but the customers were subdued. The card games seemed to have little life in them. The men lining the bar did their drinking silently. Everybody worked hard at not looking directly at Slade and Morgan. At a far table Morgan recognized the skinny gunman who had slipped out of the Pony Express station. He was slumped deep in a chair, trying to be inconspicuous.

Slade strode across the sawdust-covered floor to the bar. Morgan followed a watchful two paces behind.

The bartender put on a businesslike smile. " 'Morning, gents. What'll it be?"

"Jules Reni," said Slade.

"Beg pardon?"

"I'm here to see Jules Reni." Slade pronounced the words slowly and distinctly, as to a child.

"I think Mr. Reni's in his office." The bartender was apparently going to stop right there, but he saw the look in Slade's eyes and went on quickly. "That's right at the top of the stairs."

Slade and Morgan walked past the silent man and climbed a flight of stairs to a balcony overlooking the saloon. The single door there was ajar. Slade pushed it open and they walked in.

The room had an expensive carpet on the floor and a big crystal chandelier. There was overstuffed leather furniture with brass studs. From one wall the stuffed head of a moose looked down on them with glassy gaze.

Behind a polished mahogany desk Jules Reni sat in a high-backed swivel chair with a fat black cigar clenched in his teeth. His expanse of chest and belly made him look as broad as the desk. A smile flashed toothy and white under the sooty moustache.

"Ah, this would be the famous Captain Slade."

Slade acknowledged it with a fractional nod.

"I have heard many stories of your adventures in the war and afterward. It is my pleasure to meet you at long last."

Reni stuck out a bearpaw of a hand. Slade ignored it, keeping his eyes on the other man's face.

"I'm not here on a pleasure trip," he said.

"Ah, business then." Reni's eyes, small and black, flicked over to Morgan. "The young man is here on the same business?"

"That's right. This is Morgan Bunker of the Pony Express."

"Well, then," said Reni with a show of geniality, "we are all working for the same company."

Slade did not return the smile. "Morgan and I are working for the Central Overland. There is some question in Mr. Russell's mind about whom you're working for."

The smile stayed in place around the cigar, but the Frenchman's black little eyes hardened. "I don't think I understand you."

"There's been some worrisome reports about the way the Pony Express operation is being run in Julesburg."

"Reports? What reports?"

"It seems there is some question about where the money is going. The money the Central Overland gives you to run the station here."

"It is not cheap to keep things running smoothly."

"It's a lot cheaper if you cut corners on provisions for the riders and caring for the stock."

Reni took the cigar out of his mouth and set it daintily on the edge of a big copper ashtray. The smile faded. "Who is saying these things about my station?"

"Word has come from the riders."

"It is not true, none of the things you say. I run a first-class operation in Julesburg. Why would the riders want to lie about me?"

"I asked myself the same question, and I can't see where they'd have a reason in the world."

"Either they lied, or they made a mistake."

"Maybe. Do you have any objections if Morgan and I have a look around for ourselves?"

"Why should I have objections? Look around all you want."

"We'll talk later," said Slade.

Morgan walked back down the stairs with Slade, conscious of the watching eyes on them from all corners of the room. Slade gave no sign that he noticed, and they made their way back out into the sunlight.

"Where do we start?" Morgan asked. "Back at the Pony station?"

"We'll get there," said Slade. "First I want to take a look at the stock."

They walked around in back of the office to the corral. At the splintering fence they stopped and surveyed the dozen or so horses inside. The animals showed no interest in the men, but continued to munch apathetically at piles of dusty brown hay.

"What do you think, Morgan?" Slade asked.

"That's a sorry-lookin' example of horseflesh. Worse than anything I've seen at the other Pony stations."

"That's what I thought too."

A gnarled man with a crippled right hand sat nearby on a nail keg. He was laboriously sharpening a sickle blade with a whetstone, and paid no attention to the two strangers.

Slade walked over to him. "Who's the head wrangler around here?"

The man continued rubbing the whetstone along the sickle blade. "You're lookin' at him."

"Then stand up so I can get a good look."

The snap of authority in Slade's voice brought the man out of his lethargy. He quickly put the sickle blade aside and got up off the nail keg. "Is there somethin' I can do for you?"

"I was wondering where you keep the grain for those horses."

"Grain?"

"To mix with their feed."

"Hell, they got all the hay they want. What do they need grain for?"

"Who do you take your orders from?" Slade asked.

"Jules Reni, like everybody else around here."

"Is it Reni's orders that you feed these horses on hay alone?"

"Sure it is." The old man cocked his head to one side and squinted. "Who are you, anyhow, mister?"

"The name is Slade. Captain Jack Slade."

The wrangler's jaw dropped. He remained standing there with his mouth hanging open as Slade and Morgan headed for the station.

When they entered this time they found Amos Ingram alert and busy-looking at the desk. The card table had been dismantled, and the players were nowhere in sight.

"Howdy, Captain Slade. Did you meet up with Mr. Reni all right?"

"I found him," Slade said. "What I want now is a look at your books."

"Books?"

"Don't people around here understand English? I want to see the account books where you keep a record of the money that comes in from Russell and Company, and the money that's spent for supplies and such. I presume you *do* keep such a record."

"Oh, right, sure we do." Ingram put on an apologetic smile. "The thing is, we keep them books locked up. I don't know if Mr. Reni'd want me to get 'em out."

"Do you want me to go get Jules Reni and bring him back here to give you a direct order?"

"No, sir, Captain Slade, you don't hafta do that," Ingram said quickly. "I'm sure it'll be all right, you bein' with the company and all."

"Then get to it."

Ingram sprang out of his chair and scurried to a locked cabinet at the rear of the room. With an eager smile at Slade, he fumbled through a ring of keys and found one to open the padlock holding the cabinet doors. He poked through a pile of papers inside, deftly sliding out a ledger book. As he started to close the cabinet Slade spoke up.

"What about that other book?"

"Other book?"

Slade turned to Morgan with an air of nonchalance. "If I have to repeat myself one more time to somebody who's standing right in front of me, I might have to rearrange somebody's ears."

"Oh, you mean *this* other book," Ingram said, quickly locating a mate to the first ledger.

"Yes, that one," Slade said drily.

"It's just a copy of the other one. I think."

"If you don't mind, I'll just take both books along with me for a little while," Slade said. "You *don't* mind, do you?"

"Oh, no, Captain Slade. Not me."

"Good. Let's go, Morgan."

They crossed the street to the Julesburg Hotel where Slade rented a room. For the rest of the day he sat at the writing table studying the two account books and making pages of notes in his neat handwriting. For a while Morgan tried to follow the columns of figures and the handwritten entries in the account books, but gave up when he could make no sense out of them.

Finally Slade clapped the last of the ledger books shut. He leaned back in the chair and lit a long thin cigar.

"Find anything fishy?" Morgan asked.

"It's just like Bill Russell suspected," said Slade. "Jules Reni is robbing the Central Overland just like he did in the old days, only now he's doing it with a pen instead of a gun."

There was a rap at the door.

Slade stood up and buckled on his gunbelt without any undue haste. With his eyes he signaled Morgan to stand on the other side of the room.

"Who is it?"

"Jules Reni."

"Come on in."

The door opened and the stocky Frenchman entered. Behind him was the sallow-faced gunman who had slipped out of the poker game to warn him of Slade's arrival.

"Hello, Reni," said Slade. "We were just talking about you."

The black little eyes took in the two ledger books lying on the table. "You been doing some reading, I see."

"That's right. It's surprising what a man can learn from books."

"For instance?"

"For instance, that you're a thief."

The room went dead silent, the air crackling with tension. Reni's gunman flexed his fingers, but relaxed at a quick look from his boss.

"Another man would have died for calling me that," Reni said.

Jack Slade did not blink. "If you can prove I'm a liar, I'll apologize. If you can't, you're in considerable trouble."

Reni's eyes flickered across Morgan. "Can we talk about it? Just the two of us?"

Slade shook his head. "Morgan and I are working together."

Reni shrugged. A semblance of his old smile returned. He jerked his thumb at the thin gunman. "Wait for me outside, Yancey."

He waited until the door was closed before he spoke again. "May I sit down?"

"Suit yourself."

Reni settled himself into an upholstered chair. He pulled one of the fat cigars from his breast pocket, offered another to Slade.

"No, thanks."

As an afterthought, Reni held out a cigar toward Morgan, who shook his head.

The Frenchman took his time lighting up and blowing a cloud of gray smoke at the ceiling. "So. You say you found some, well, mistakes in our bookkeeping."

"No mistakes, Reni," Slade told him. "More like deliberate thievery."

Reni's eyes snapped angrily, but he held onto his composure. "What is your next move?"

"To make my report to Mr. Russell."

"I suppose you know that would make a great deal of trouble for me."

"I guess that's your outlook, isn't it?"

"Are you willing to listen to an offer?"

"Spell it out."

Reni seemed to regain some of his old confidence. "As I presume you saw in the accounts, this station has been quite a profitable venture."

"So I noticed."

"There is, in fact, enough to provide a generous share for you."

Slade nodded, the bullet eyes unreadable. "What would I have to do for it?"

"Merely say in your report that you found nothing out of order in Julesburg."

"Do I understand that you're asking me to lie to William Russell and the Central Overland?"

The Frenchman shifted uneasily in his chair. Some

of the confidence slipped away. "Come on, Jack, we can be straight with each other. I know the stories about you. You are never accused of being a saint."

"Maybe not," Slade said, "but another thing I'm never accused of is cheating the man who pays me."

Reni struggled to his feet and stood glaring at Slade, the cigar clenched in his teeth.

"One more thing. There are maybe half a dozen people in the world who I like well enough to let them call me Jack. You aren't one of them."

"You're making a big mistake," Reni told him.

"The mistake is yours, Reni. You owned this whole town. You had everything you could possibly want here. But you got greedy and thought you could cheat the Central Overland. Well, you got caught, and now you're through."

"You can't do anything to me. In Julesburg I am the law."

"Not any more, you're not. You got in over your head this time."

Reni curled his lip scornfully. "What are you going to do now, arrest me?"

"That's not my job," Slade told him calmly. "I was sent here to find where the trouble was. I found it. If you want some advice, clear out. Now."

Very slowly Reni took the cigar out of his mouth. He dropped it to the carpet and ground it under his heel. "I'm sorry we couldn't strike a deal, *Captain* Slade. I think you will be sorry too."

Morgan opened the door for him, and with heavy dignity the Frenchman walked out of the room.

"Do you think he really will clear out?" Morgan asked.

"Not likely. Reni's had too good a thing going here for too long to give up easy. The only way he'll leave

Julesburg is feet first." He compressed his lips in what passed for a smile from Jack Slade. "But that's not our problem. Not this trip. Let's go get ourselves a good meal, grab some shuteye, and be ready to catch the westbound stage in the morning. I don't think it will be healthy for us to hang around Julesburg any longer than we have to."

They went across the street to the Crystal Cafe and ate a leisurely dinner of roast pork with green peas, fried potatoes, and hot corn bread. Morgan washed his down with a beer, but Captain Slade drank only coffee. Morgan began to wonder if the stories of his hard drinking were exaggerated.

When they left the restaurant the sun was down and a twilight gloom lay over the town. The street was empty of people. Down in front of the Buckskin Saloon several horses jigged nervously at the hitching rail.

As they walked back across the street Slade said in a low voice, "Keep your eyes open. Something doesn't feel right."

All his senses alert, Morgan walked slowly across the expanse of rutted dirt next to Slade. The street seemed to have grown wide as the Missouri River. They at last reached the boardwalk in front of the hotel, and Morgan began to relax when he saw something move.

It was a shadow that detached itself from the darkness between the hotel and a barber shop. The shadow became a man with a revolver in his hand. At the same instant an explosion boomed from the other direction. Morgan heard Slade grunt in surprise as he drew his Colt and fired in a single continuous motion.

The gunman howled in pain as his own pistol discharged into the ground. He melted back into the darkness to the sound of running feet.

Morgan whirled to see Jack Slade sprawled awkwardly in the dirt. Beyond him, some twenty yards away, a man with a scattergun was struggling to reload. Morgan took careful aim this time and fired. The shotgunner clutched at his throat, letting the weapon fall to the ground. He gave one gargling cry, staggered backward two steps, and fell.

Morgan stood over the fallen Slade. His eyes flicked up and down the deserted street, but there was no immediate threat.

People began to come cautiously out of the hotel to see what was happening. Still holding his pistol, Morgan knelt beside the motionless man in the dirt.

20

"ARE you hurt bad, Captain Slade?" Morgan asked.

A small crowd of people now stood along the walk in front of the hotel, looking down at the two men.

Slade lay motionless, and Morgan began to fear he was dead. Then he raised his head slightly to look up at Morgan.

"Of all the Goddamned embarrassing things . . . the sonofabitch shot me in the ass."

Somebody laughed. Slade glared up at the crowd and the laughter died.

"Did you get him?" he asked Morgan.

"I got him. I think I winged another one, too. I just wish I'd seen 'em quicker."

"Hell, I didn't see them at all until I got hit with the buckshot. I must be getting old."

"Well, it was dark . . ."

"Don't make excuses for me. Give me a hand up."

"Can you walk all right?"

"We'll soon find out."

Grasping Morgan's outstretched hand, Slade pulled himself gingerly to his feet. He looked down at the dead shotgunner, then at the splintered wooden pillar a few feet away in front of the hotel.

"The sonofabitch was some rotten shot to miss killing me at that range. Let's go find somebody to pick these pellets out of my ass."

With one hand on Morgan's shoulder for support, Slade managed to walk into the hotel. He ignored the stares from the citizens as they crossed the lobby to the desk where a baldheaded little clerk ogled at them through a pair of thick spectacles.

Morgan said, "We'll need a doctor up in our room right away."

"I don't know," the clerk said doubtfully. "It could be hard to find Doc Fletcher this time of night."

Slade let go of Morgan's shoulder and planted both hands on the desk. He leaned forward, bringing his face close to the clerk's.

"You go find that doctor, little man, or he's going to have more than one patient to look after."

"Y-yes, *sir*," the clerk stammered. "I think I know where he might be." He edged around the desk and scurried out of the hotel. Slade glared around the lobby, and the bystanders melted away.

They walked back across the lobby and Morgan assisted Slade up the flight of stairs to the room they had rented. Once inside Slade stretched out face-down on the bed. He cursed steadily in a low monotone.

"Is there anything I can do to make you easier?" Morgan asked.

"Yes," Slade ground out between clenched teeth. "Bring me whiskey."

"I saw a saloon the other side of the barber shop," Morgan said. "I'll run right down and get a bottle."

"Not *a* bottle," Slade said. "I don't want to run out early."

"Got you, Captain," Morgan said. He started out of the room.

"Morgan."

He turned back. Slade rolled painfully over on one side to look at him.

"I think we've been through enough together now that you ought to start calling me Jack."

Morgan grinned at him and nodded. "I'll go see about that whiskey."

As he went through the lobby, clusters of people stood around talking in low, excited voices. Morgan felt a little thrill of pride at the new respect they showed him.

As he headed for the door Morgan almost ran into the bespectacled little clerk rushing back in. With him was a grumpy-looking man carrying a black satchel.

"Here's Doc Fletcher," the clerk said. To the doctor: "This is Mr. Bunker. He's here with Captain Slade."

The doctor grunted an acknowledgment. "Where's the patient?"

"Up in the room. He's waiting for you."

"How's he doing?" asked the clerk.

"He's in a surly mood," Morgan said. "I can tell you that much."

"Oh, dear," said the clerk. "We'd better get up there right away."

Morgan watched the two men start up the stairs, then he went back out onto the street. The body of the shotgunner had been taken away, and the night was silent again, except for the noise that came from several saloons along the length of the street. Morgan went into the nearest one, two doors from the hotel.

The conversation died in front of him as he crossed the room, to pick up again once he had passed. It was like walking within a bubble of silence, a mark of the respect he had gained since the shooting. It was a taste of the loneliness Jack Slade lived with, and Morgan felt a surprising twinge of pity for the man.

The bartender smiled at him, eager to please. "What can I do for you, sir?"

"Two bottles of your best rye whiskey." As the bartender selected the bottles off a shelf behind the bar, Morgan added, "Better make it three."

He returned to the hotel room to find Jack Slade still prone on the bed. His pants were off and his union suit cut away to expose his pale buttocks and upper thighs. The doctor stood over Slade with a sponge in one hand and a basin of pink-tinted water in the other. The hotel clerk, looking nervous, stood back against the wall, deliberately keeping his eyes averted. Morgan approached the bed. He could see a half-dozen small wounds where the buckshot pellets had penetrated the skin.

"Your friend was lucky," Dr. Fletcher said. "He just caught the edge of the buckshot pattern. An inch or so better aim with the scattergun and we'd have nothing here but an oozy corpse."

"Just get the lead out of my tail," Slade told him. "You can tell people all about it later."

The doctor put away the sponge and basin. He opened the satchel and selected a thin-bladed scalpel and forceps with a long needle nose. He uncorked a bottle of alcohol and splashed it over the wounded area. Slade winced.

"This is likely to smart a bit," the doctor warned. "I might have to go in pretty deep to dig out some of those pellets."

"Just do it and get it over with," Slade said. He turned his head toward Morgan. "Did you get the whiskey?"

"Right here."

"Well, let's have it."

Morgan pulled the cork from one of the bottles and started for the bureau, where there was a pitcher and a couple of water glasses.

"Never mind the glass," Slade said. "Just hand over the jug."

He took the bottle from Morgan and raised his head to take a long pull. Some of the whiskey spilled on the bed.

"Well, what are you waiting for, sawbones? Do what you're getting paid to do."

During the next hour, while the doctor worked on his wounds, Slade emptied the first bottle of whiskey and called for the second. He had become increasingly silent, responding only with a grunt when the doctor probed especially deep.

At last Dr. Fletcher tweezed out the last of the pellets and dropped it into a tin cup and rattled it. "That should do it. Eight little hunks of lead. You should be all right as long as you don't get blood poisoning."

"A little bit of lead isn't going to poison me," Slade assured him.

The doctor spread a thick yellow salve over the raw flesh. "You won't sit so comfortable for the next few days, but all things considered, I'd say you came out pretty lucky."

"Luckier than the man who shot me," Slade said, unsmiling. "And luckier than the man who sent him too."

Dr. Fletcher looked uncomfortable. "I wouldn't know about that."

Slade eased off the bed. He pulled up his pants. "How much do I owe you?"

"Ten dollars will cover it."

"Isn't that a mite steep?"

"It is if you think you could have done the job yourself."

Slade paid him without further conversation. The doctor collected the desk clerk, who seemed vastly relieved, and left the room.

Slade walked stiffly across the room to the window and looked out at the darkness. His face had the look of a gathering storm. The bullet eyes glittered in a way that made Morgan decidedly uneasy.

"Are we still plannin' to catch the morning stage out of town?" he asked.

"You can if you want to," said Slade, still looking out the window. "I've got some unfinished business in Julesburg."

"We was sent here to do a job together," Morgan said. "I don't aim to leave till it's finished."

"It strikes me that you've done more than your share of the job already, but suit yourself. Hand me that other bottle."

Slade remained standing at the window. He drank whiskey from the bottle in a steady, purposeful way. Morgan sat down to relax for a minute in the armchair, and before he knew it, he dozed off.

He awoke with a start, and it took a moment for him to remember where he was. Then he saw Jack Slade across the room buckling on his guns. The three empty whiskey bottles stood neatly against the wall. Morgan jumped up and grabbed his own gunbelt. What he could see of the morning through the window was gray and cold. He wished he was back in California.

Jack Slade walked somewhat stiff-legged from the buckshot wounds, but his hand was steady and his eyes were clear, showing no evidence of last night's drinking. Morgan had never seen a man put away that much whiskey and remain standing.

Slade shrugged into the black frock coat and adjusted the planter's hat square on his head.

"Shall we go?" he asked.

"I'm ready," Morgan said.

They went downstairs together. As they passed the desk a new clerk smiled brightly. "Enjoying your stay, gents?"

Slade glared at him, and the man looked like he wanted to crawl under the desk.

"Sorry, Captain Slade, I wasn't thinking." When he got no response, the man rattled on. "I don't want you to worry none about the shooting last night. Neither of you. Everybody saw it was self-defense. That's what we'll tell the federal marshal when he comes around." He paused and was still met with silence. "I, uh, suppose you'll be leaving on the morning stage?"

"We're not finished here," Slade told him. The tone of his voice shut the man up.

Slade and Morgan walked down the street to the Pony Express station. The door was locked. Across the street someone came out of a feed store, then turned quickly and started to go back in.

"Hold it," Slade called, freezing the man in his tracks.

As they crossed the street Morgan recognized the man as Yancey, Jules Reni's sallow gunman. He wore a fresh bandage on his right wrist.

Slade did not stop until he stood directly in front of Yancey, a hand's breadth away. The thin gunman tried to meet the bullet gaze, but could not do it.

"Hurt yourself?" Slade said.

"Cut my arm on some barb wire."

"Too bad. Where's Reni?"

"I don't know."

"I'm going to ask you politely one more time. Where is Jules Reni?"

"I don't know. That's the truth."

With a move faster than Morgan could follow, Slade had his Army Colt .44 out of the holster with the muzzle jammed up against the gunman's nose. Yancey's eyes crossed as he stared at the gun. Slade shoved the barrel up his nostril, tearing out a good chunk of flesh with the front sight.

"Where's Reni?"

"He'll kill me," Yancey whined as the blood trickled down over his lips.

Slade thumbed back the hammer of the Colt. "Better stand away, Morgan, so you don't get brains on you."

Yancey made a little squealing sound. "He's in a cabin a mile north of town on the Dry Creek Road. It's behind a clump of trees, so you gotta look sharp."

"Is he alone?"

"Yeah. I was gonna ride out and tell him if you left on the stage."

"Well, I guess I'll just ride out and deliver that message myself."

Slade took the gun out of Yancey's nose and eased the hammer down. He said, "I don't know why, Yancey, but I'm going to let you live."

The gunman's knees buckled and he almost sagged to the ground.

"But if I see your face again I'm going to shoot it off. Understand?"

Yancey bobbed his head up and down, unable to speak.

Slade spun on his heel and strode back across the street without looking back. Morgan kept a sidelong eye on Yancey, but the gunman was in no shape to do anything hostile. He just sagged against the wall of the feed store and wiped with his bandana at the blood trickling out of his ripped-open nose.

"Let's get ourselves a couple of mounts and make tracks," said Slade. "I don't reckon Jules Reni will stay put very long."

They found the livery stable at the lower end of the street and hired a pair of horses. They rode back through Julesburg and out the wagon trail to the north that was called Dry Creek Road. After ten minutes they spotted a thick grove of blue spruce. They approached cautiously and saw a log cabin nestled back in the trees. Slade held up a hand and they reined to a stop.

"Do you think he's in there, Jack?" Morgan said.

"If he isn't, I'm going back and kill that skinny gunslinger."

"What do we do, rush the cabin?"

"Not *we*, me. This is my fight from here on. You cover my rear in case there's anybody hiding in the trees. That snake Yancey said Reni was here alone, but I'm not ready to stake my life on his word."

Slade dismounted and covered the ground to the grove of trees in a crouching, zig-zagging run. He showed no ill effects of the recent wound. Morgan unholstered his Colt and scanned the trees and the surrounding countryside. All was still. Slade turned to look back at him. Morgan gave him a nod.

Moving with remarkable agility, Slade approached the cabin darting from tree to tree. Morgan marveled that a man with three quarts of whiskey and, until recently, eight buckshot pellets in him could move like that. When he came to the last of the trees, ten yards from the cabin door, Slade drew his guns. He stood sideways, using the tree trunk to shield as much of his body as possible.

"Reni!" he called. "This is Captain Slade. Come out of there or I'm coming in after you."

The answer was a gunshot from the cabin window. The slug chipped a hunk of bark off the tree where Slade was standing. He spun into the open and fired both pistols. The flap of hide covering the window danced as two bullets punched it.

Without hesitation, Slade sprinted to the door of the cabin, raised a booted foot, and kicked it open. Morgan watched him disappear into the dark interior.

The horses whinnied and shied at the gunfire. Morgan seized the reins of Slade's mount and made soothing sounds. A fusillade of muffled gunshots boomed inside the cabin. A male voice roared in pain or in anger. Then two more shots.

At last it was quiet. A breeze from the north brought the sharp smell of cordite to Morgan's nose. He waited, wondering whether he should enter the cabin.

Just as he had decided to go down and take a look, Jack Slade walked out through the door. His guns were holstered, and he was carrying something wrapped in a bandana. Morgan watched him stride resolutely through the trees.

When he reached the spot where Morgan waited with the horses, Slade swung aboard his mount without speaking. The look on his face warned Morgan that this was no time to ask questions. There was really nothing to ask, anyway. When Jack Slade walked out of the cabin alone, there could be no doubt about the condition of the man still inside.

They rode the mile back to Julesburg in silence.

Slade held the reins with one hand, using the other to carry whatever he had wrapped in the bandana.

The street was lined with people who had heard through the magical communication of the West that a gunfight had taken place. They stared curiously at the two riders. Slade kept his eyes straight ahead. Morgan noticed that the gunman Yancey was conspicuously absent.

They rode to the livery stable and returned the horses. A crowd of citizens followed at a respectful distance.

"I'd like to borrow a hammer and a nail," Slade told the stable hand. It was the first time he had spoken since coming out of the cabin.

"Just one nail?"

"That will be enough."

The stable hand scouted up a hammer and a heavy three-inch nail and turned them over to Slade. He then joined the crowd that followed Morgan and the tall gunfighter as they left the stable and walked back up the street.

Slade came to a stop at the Pony Express station. While the crowd edged closer, he carefully unwrapped the bandana he had carried back from the cabin. He removed two bloody scraps of tissue. Holding them one atop the other, he drove the nail through them into the wood of the door panel.

Morgan turned away and walked with Slade back toward the hotel. Behind them the crowd closed in silently for a better look at Jules Reni's ears.

21

By 1860 the wild, unhibited days of the gold rush were just a memory in San Francisco. Most of the hardy breed of forty-niners had gone broke and gone home, or they had gone broke and stayed on, finding other ways of making a living. A few had found a fortune and kept it and built fine mansions on the scenic hills of the city. And many of the merchants, the bankers, and the professionals who got rich off the miners remained.

The bay teemed with ships from all ports of the world. The old bawdy houses, the gambling dens, the rowdy saloons had not been eliminated, but they had been removed to designated parts of the city where they would not offend the eyes of genteel ladies and impressionable children.

A source of pride for the new San Francisco was its collection of fine resturants where world-famous chefs prepared gourmet meals for those who could afford them. One such restaurant was Les Centimes on Montgomery Street.

In a private alcove upstairs in Les Centimes, curtained off from the other diners, Jessie McKee enjoyed a meal of wild duck and fresh oysters. Next to her sat an extremely uncomfortable Cherokee Joe Bunker. Across the table was Andrew Nagle, an assistant to the Postmaster General in President Buchanan's cabinet. Nagle, a portly man with gray muttonchop whiskers, did his best to ignore Cherokee Joe, directing his conversation to Jessie, who at least looked like she belonged there.

"As I've told you," Nagle said, "I am continuing to advise Postmaster General Holt to go slow in awarding any mail contract to Russell and his partners. So far, he has been content to wait and see."

"I still don't see any signs of the Pony Express going out of business," Jessie said.

"Unfortunately," Nagle said, "the operation continues to show remarkable success. There is pressure from the senate that makes it more difficult every day to withhold the contract."

Jessie's eyes turned cold. "Nagle, I'm paying you a lot of money to see to it that there is no mail contract given to the Central Overland. You assured me that Joseph Holt wouldn't make a move without your approval."

"I don't believe I put it as strongly as that," Nagle protested.

Cherokee Joe drined his glass of wine and wiped his mouth with the back of his hand. "What Miz McKee is tellin' you, Nagle, is that you are suckin' a heap of money out her company, and she expects you to deliver the goods."

Nagle looked at Joe as though he were speaking a foreign language. "I beg your pardon?"

"Don't look down your nose at me, mister," Joe

warned. "A politician who takes bribes got no call to think he's better'n anybody."

"That's enough, Joe," Jessie said.

Nagle turned to her. "Does this man have to be here?"

"He is here at my invitation," Jessie said, "and if sometimes he speaks a little rough, he still speaks for me. What I want from you is suggestions on how we can hobble the Pony Express, and I want them now."

Nagle glanced around uneasily. "I do have something for you, but if word were ever to get out I gave you this information . . ."

"Neither Joe Bunker nor I are given to loose talk," Jessie told him. "Let's hear what you have."

"You know they are greatly concerned in Washington about the pro-South feeling here in California. They worry about which side California would take if the southern states make good their threat to secede."

"So I hear," Jessie said.

"Even though it was admitted as a free state, there are a lot of southerners out here. And Senator Gwin makes no secret of his sympathies for the South."

"I know all that, Nagle," Jessie prompted. "Get to the point."

"It's the feeling in Washington that if the economy of California were based on Federal paper money, the state would be compelled to side with the Union in case of a war."

Cherokee Joe's lip curled. "Paper money? You mean they expect us to trade our gold for shin plasters?"

"I'm not talking about that five and ten-cent stuff, I mean the real thing. Big bills. Greenbacks. Within a few years the whole country will be on paper money."

"All right, what's the plan?" Jessie said.

"The treasury is going to ship a considerable sum in

greenbacks to California banks to replace their gold reserves."

"I don't see what that has to do with us," Jessie said.

Nagle leaned across the table and lowered his voice. "Because they feel the situation is urgent, the treasury people want to delivery the first shipment of greenbacks the fastest way they can get them here. That means by Pony Express."

"You ain't never gonna get folks in the west to go for no greenbacks," Joe said. "Out here we like money that clinks in a man's pocket."

Jessie silenced him with a look, then returned her attention to Nagle. "Just how much money is coming in this first shipment of greenbacks?"

Nagle answered deliberately, emphasizing each word. "One . . . million . . . dollars."

Cherokee Joe whistled appreciatively. "There ain't that much money."

"I assure you there is," Nagle said. "They plan to issue 150 million dollars' worth by next year, so this represents a considerable portion."

Jessie looked thoughtful. "If the Pony Express comes through and delivers this bundle of money for the Federal Government, it will be tough to keep the Central Overland from getting the mail contract."

"It will be virtually impossible," said Nagle.

"On the other hand," Jessie went on, "if something should go wrong, if the Pony Express should somehow lose that million dollars, it would leave Bill Russell and his partners in deep trouble."

"It would certainly hurt their case in Washington," Nagle agreed.

"So what we have to do is make sure that million dollars never gets where it's supposed to go."

Nagle coughed into his fist and glanced nervously at the curtains. "I don't want to know anything about that."

"Don't worry," Jessie told him, "you won't be involved. All I'll need from you is the date the greenbacks leave St. Joseph by Pony."

"I can get you that."

"Good. Now if you don't want to hear any more details that might upset you, I suggest you leave now and head back to your hotel."

Nagle pushed his chair back from the table and stood up hastily. "Yes, thank you, you're right. I do hope you understand why I cannot become involved in the, er, mechanics of your operation."

"I understand," Jessie said drily. "You just keep doing your job in Washington and get me the date of the greenback shipment. I've got other people working for me who can handle the mechanics."

Andrew Nagle parted the velvet curtains, looked around outside, then left quickly. An unfinished plum cake dessert remained on his plate.

"I don't trust that fat dude," Joe said when he and Jessie were alone.

"We don't have to trust him," Jessie said. "He knows if he doesn't play square I can ruin him."

Joe grunted noncommittally. "Reckon we could get some more of this here wine? It ain't half bad."

"Some other time," Jessie said. "Right now I want to think about how we're going to relieve the Pony Express of all that money."

"You really mean we're goin' to go out and steal one million dollars?"

"What the hell do you think, that I'm going to ask old man Russell politely to hand it over?"

"Whooee! I never once stole more'n a thousand at

one crack." Joe sobered suddenly. "This ain't gonna mean shootin' down any Pony riders?"

"Not if I can help it," Jessie said. "The less blood spilled the better."

"Usually I got no feelin's about shootin' a man when you got to, but this is a little different."

"I know your boy Morgan rides for the Pony, Joe, but chances are he won't be anywhere near when we pull the job. Anyway, you better be straight in your head about which side you're on."

"I'm on your side, Jessie, you know that. Morgan chose the road he wanted to follow, and I reckon he can take care of hisself. I just don't want to see none of them young fellers killed if we don't have to."

"Fair enough," Jessie said. She drummed her laquered fingernails on the tablecloth. "We'd better leave now. I'm going to have to spend some time planning how we're going to do this so everybody will know what his job is."

Joe reached under the table and squeezed her leg hard above the knee. "Before you get all busied up makin' plans for everybody, what say you and me make them bed slats creak."

"God, you can be crude," she said.

"And don't you love it."

Jessie gave him a fierce scowl that dissolved into a smile. "You do know me, you mangy wolf."

"I ought to by this time," he said. "Let's quit wastin' time and get on up to your room."

"Let's," Jessie said. She parted the velvet curtains and led the way out.

A mile away the new big houses on Telegraph Hill overlooked the embarcadero. The houses were widely separated by expanses of green lawn and neat groves of trees. Seated on a blanket laid flat in one of these park-like stretches were Beth Catlin and Jack Bunker. Beth was gazing thoughtfully down at the black water of the bay while Jack gazed only at Beth.

"What are you thinkin' about?" he asked.

"I was just wondering whether my mother and your father will ever get married."

"I don't know about your ma," Jack said, "but I'd have to think it's mighty unlikely that Pa will marry up with anybody again."

"I guess he doesn't have a very high opinion of women."

"It ain't that so much. Pa just don't think a man ought to get hisself all tied up legal to one woman. No offense to your ma. If Pa *was* to take a wife, I've no doubt she'd be the one."

"If they did get married, that would make us kind of brother and sister. Not by blood, of course, but by marriage."

Jack shook his head. "I couldn't feel like no brother to you, no matter what."

Beth peeked up at him through her thick blonde lashes. "Why not, Jack? Don't you like me enough?"

"I like you too all-fired much. But not in the way a brother is supposed to like his sister."

Beth answered him with a quiet smile. She turned away again to watch the ships in the harbor below.

"Fact is," Jack continued, "I've been meanin' to talk to you."

He was silent for several seconds. Finally Beth said "Go ahead, Jack."

"I was wonderin' if you and me couldn't have us a, well, an understandin' of sorts."

"What do you mean?"

"I mean, doggone it, I want you and me to be, you know, special."

"Are you asking me to be your sweetheart?"

Jack sat for a moment tearing up little chunks of grass, then he turned suddenly. "That's what I'm sayin'."

Beth reached over and took his hand. "That's awfully sweet of you, Jack. I do like you an awful lot, but I could never feel that way about you."

"Well, why not?"

"I guess if I hadn't met someone else first, it might have been different."

"You mean Morgan?"

Beth dropped her gaze for a moment, then looked back into his eyes. "Yes, it's Morgan. When I'm with him I feel something different from anything I've ever known. I feel all weak and giddy and really, truly alive. I want to laugh and cry all at the same time. Am I making any sense?"

Jack turned away from her. "Not very much."

"You're really a nice boy, Jack, and you and I will always be special friends."

"I'm only a year younger'n Morgan."

"You will always be my friend, won't you?"

"Oh, I reckon." Jack continued to stare gloomily out toward the shadowy line where the ocean met the sky. His eyes were unreadable.

Beth shivered and hugged her shoulders. "It's getting chilly up here. Maybe we'd better go."

Jack stood up. Beth waited a moment for him to offer a hand. When he did not, she got to her feet. Jack folded up the blanket and they walked together down the hill in silence.

22

THE middle months of 1860 were a time of turmoil for the nation. The southern states were becoming louder and more militant in their threats to leave the Union. Indeed, there were rumors that South Carolina would actually secede before the end of the year if the Republican anti-slavery candidate, Abraham Lincoln, were elected president. And to the surprise of many, Lincoln's strength with the voters seemed to be increasing.

The Pony Express continued its spectacular success in delivering the mail. By the end of its second month of operation, 24 hours had been shaved from the St. Joseph-to-Sacramento run. The riders were making two trips a week in each direction, and the cost of letters carried by the Pony had been dropped from five dollars per half-ounce to one dollar. From a business standpoint, however, the Central Overland was not doing so well.

There still had been no action on awarding the mail contract. Both President Buchanan and Postmaster General Holt were strangely silent. William Russell was forced to dig deeply into the resources of the Central Overland's freight business to make up for the deficit shown by the Pony Express. Partner William Waddell withdrew his support completely. Andrew Majors stayed on only with great reluctance.

Portents of trouble for the Pony Express were everywhere. In Utah Territory raids by the hostile Paiutes had increased to a point where a full-blown war seemed inevitable. Also, telegraph poles were starting to go up west of Missouri along the route covered by the Pony riders. Everyone knew that once the wires were up, the days of the mounted mail carriers would be over.

Still, the glamor of the Pony Express was undiminished. Young men clamored for the few jobs made available by riders leaving the company. William Russell clung to his dream and waited for the word from Washington.

One bright spot for the Central Overland was the improved operation in Julesburg following the visit by Jack Slade and Morgan Bunker. The two men quietly accepted the thanks of their firm, then parted company. Slade took a leave of absence and headed for Texas, where he said he had personal business to attend to. Nobody asked him for details. Morgan returned to his former station at Three Fools Creek to resume riding his lap between there and Carson City.

He found the route was now regularly patrolled by soldiers on the lookout for maurading Indians. The relay stations were more heavily armed now in Paiute country, and everybody was a little bit nervous.

Morgan was surprised when, during the heat of August, Bolivar Roberts rode into the station at Three Fools.

"How's it going, Morgan?" he asked as the two strolled together in the cool desert evening.

"No problems, Mr. Roberts."

"The Paiutes been keeping their distance, have they?"

"So far. It's right comfortin' to know the army's close by in case of trouble, but to tell you the truth, it takes a good deal of the excitement out of the ride."

"It might at that," Roberts agreed. "I've been talking to Mr. Russell about shifting you boys around from time to time. Give you a chance to see different parts of the country."

"That could be a good idea," Morgan said. "A man tends to get careless when he does the same thing, or rides the same trail over and over."

"That's what I thought." Mr. Russell has other problems, and he isn't completely sold on the idea yet. But I do have a new assignment for you, if you want it."

"I'm willin' to listen."

"How would you like to take the run from Placerville into Sacramento?"

"The last leg?"

"Right."

"That'd be quite an honor."

"The company thinks mighty highly of you, Morgan."

"I'm glad to hear that."

"We're right proud of the way you came through with those bushwhackers in Stillwater Notch, and they're still talking about how you helped clean out the mess in Julesburg."

"That was mostly Captain Slade's doin'."

"Never mind being so all-fired modest, boy. I've

seen Jack Slade's report, and he gives you a goodly share of the credit."

"Well," Morgan said, "if that's what it says in the Captain's report, I better not deny it."

"That's more like it," Roberts said. "When you know you've done a good piece of work, don't be bashful about admitting it. There's always plenty of others ready to take credit for what you've done."

"I'll remember that," Morgan said.

"Good. The fact is, there's a little more to this new assignment than just carrying the mail the last fifty miles."

"Oh?"

"You'll be carrying a very special package in the mochila. It's a Federal Government shipment that's mighty important both to the nation and to the Pony Express."

"Well, what is it, for mercy sake?"

"That I can't tell you," Roberts said. "Not until the package is safely delivered. But only our best and most trusted riders are being asked to handle it each step of the way."

"I can't hardly say no to that, can I?"

"Not hardly," Roberts said with a smile. "Oh, by the way, I'm supposed to tell you there's a certain young lady who will arrange to be in Sacramento when you ride in."

"Beth Catlin?" Morgan asked eagerly.

"I do believe that was the name."

"Ya*hoo!*"

"I take it that means you accept the assignment?"

"When do I start?"

"Not so fast. The date the package gets shipped out of St. Joe is still a secret, but everybody's sure it'll be soon. I just want you to be ready to go when you get the word."

"Don't you worry, Mr. Roberts, I will be."

About the time Bolivar Roberts was telling Morgan Bunker about his new assignment, Andrew Nagle in Washington was reading a confidential memorandum from the Secretary of the Treasury to the Postmaster General. After resealing the envelope, Nagle hurried to the telegraph office to send a prearranged message to the offices of Ace Freighters in St. Joseph. From there it would be forwarded to Jessie McKee in Sacramento. It read:

> *Aunt Millie leaving for California One September. Love, Uncle Joe.*

Ironically, the message would travel the last half of its journey by Pony Express.

23

CHEROKEE reined up at the top of a rise overlooking the abandoned mining camp where Jessie McKee had said they were to meet. The place would have been no bargain in the bright sunlight, but in the gloom of twilight it was downright depressing. The wooden buildings that remained from the gold rush days had never been painted, and were rapidly falling victim to the elements. Doors hung drunkenly askew on rusted hinges. Empty windows stared blindly on debris-clogged streets and splintered sidewalks.

The look of the place sent a chill down Joe's spine. The lengthening shadows seemed to hide ghosts of the miners who stripped this patch of earth of its gold and moved on in less than two years. The mine and its outbuildings had been left to the coyotes and the jackrabbits since the last diehard Forty-niner pulled out eight years ago.

Why, Joe wondered, would Jessie pick a God-forsaken place like this for the meeting? She had her reasons, he supposed, and it was really not his place to question her. All the same, he would be damn glad to get shut of the place.

He rode slowly down the grade and past the black mouth that had been the mine. He was relieved to see that Jessie was already there. He recognized her buggy out in front of one of the rickety buildings. He was not so pleased to see Smiler's blaze-faced bay tied next to the buggy. He dismounted and walked into the building.

From the look of the place, it had been a storehouse when the mine was alive. Jessie and Smiler were sitting on upended boxes waiting for him. A coal oil lamp placed on a barrel provided a circle of pale light.

"Come on in and join us," Jessie said.

"Or are you afraid of the ghosts?" Smiler said.

"I'll show you what a ghost is," Joe said. His words sounded angrier than he meant them, more because Smiler had come near the truth than for any other reason.

"Save the jawing for later," Jessie told them. "We've got important business to do tonight."

"What's it all about, anyway?" Joe asked. "And why here?"

"Because I want to be absolutely sure that nobody sees us all together, and nobody accidentally overhears what we're talking about."

"What *are* we talkin' about?" Joe asked.

Jessie held up a hand for them to be still. Outside the hoofbeats of an approaching horse could be heard. The hoofbeats stopped and spurs clinked as the rider dismounted. Joe's right hand moved automatically to his six-shooter.

"It's all right," Jessie told him. "This will be the last member of our little party."

The door squeaked open and Jack Bunker came into the building. He blinked uncertainly at the others.

"Have a seat, Jack," Jessie told him.

"I wasn't sure I come to the right place."

"This is the right place, sure enough. Now I want you boys to listen up real good, because this is the first and last time we're going to talk about this, and I want to make sure we all understand the plan."

The men glanced at each other, but kept silent, waiting for Jessie to continue.

"You might as well know right off that Ace Freighters is in serious financial trouble. I've spent a lot of money trying to keep the Central Overland from getting the cross-country mail contract, and trying to land it for us. Well, they haven't got it yet, but neither have we, and now we're damn near broke."

"You mean the company's really busted?" Smiler asked.

"Near enough. We'll meet this month's payroll, but it might be the last. That's why we're here tonight. I've got a plan that will hit the Central Overland where it hurts, and at the same time put a big chunk of money into our hands.

Jessie paused and looked briefly into the face of each of the three men. None of them had a comment, so she went on.

"Joe, you were there when Andrew Nagle told us about the shipment of greenbacks the federal government is sending to California by Pony Express. I told you about it too, Smiler. Jack, this is the first you've heard of it, but no matter, you'll learn all you have to know tonight."

"Did you find out when they're sendin' them greenbacks?" Joe asked, to show he was paying attention.

"I did. One million dollars worth leave St. Joe the

first of September. They're supposed to arrive in Sacramento on the ninth, but they won't."

"Why not?" Jack asked, then looked around, embarrassed that he had spoken.

"Because we'll have them," Jessie said.

"We heist the Pony Express?" Joe said.

"It's been tried before," Smiler said, "but nobody's pulled it off yet."

Jessie gave him a long look. "Who would know that better than you?" She let several heavy seconds go by, then she said, "But never mind, nobody has tried it the way we're going to."

"This won't involve shootin' no riders out of the saddle, will it?" Joe said. "After what happened to my boy Morgan I'm a mite touchy on that subject."

"No riders will be hurt," Jessie said. "They won't even know they've been robbed. Not until they open the lock boxes in Sacramento."

"How are we gonna manage that trick?" Smiler asked.

"That's what I'm trying to explain, if you two will kindly shut up and listen."

Cherokee Joe lit up a cheroot and blew smoke with studied nonchalance. Smiler bit off a chaw of cable twist. Jack Bunker sat leaning forward, watching the others expectantly.

"We know that once the mail is locked into the pouches in St. Joe, it's only seen three more times. They have one key to unlock the pouches at Fort Laramie, the second at Salt Lake City, and the last at the end of the run in Sacramento. After the greenbacks have been checked in Salt Lake City, and before they get to Sacramento, we take them."

"How are we goin' to do that without anybody knowin' before they get to Sacramento?" Joe asked.

Jessie knelt down too unwrap a bundle that rested at her feet. She unfolded a three-foot-square leather blanket with a heavy lock pouch in each of the four corners.

"Do you know what this is?" she asked.

"It's a Pony Express mochila," said Jack.

"You're right." Jessie smiled at him as at a bright pupil.

"Where'd you get it?" Joe asked.

"From one of the men who worked for Jules Reni up in Julesburg, before Jack Slade and your other boy cleaned out the town. His name's Yancey, and he's got a considerable grudge against the Central Overland. He brought me the mochila, and we made a deal for it."

"He ain't gonna be cut in on the plan, is he?" Smiler asked.

"Don't worry," Jessie said. "I paid him off and sent him on his way."

"You still ain't said how we're gonna go about grabbing the money," Joe said.

"I'm getting to that," Jessie said. "The first relay station for the Pony Express this side of Salt Lake is a place called White Horse Springs. According to Yancey, there isn't much there, just a 'dobe hut and a couple of horses. There are only two men on the place. What we do is send in two of us, put Russell's people out of action, and switch our mochila for theirs. The rider goes on his way none the wiser."

"What do you mean by put 'em out of action?" Joe asked.

"How the hell do I know?" Jessie said irritably. "I can't be concerned with details like that. The important thing is to get them out of sight when the rider comes in."

"Won't the rider think it's peculiar that his own people ain't there?" Smiler asked.

"Maybe, but we'll give him some kind of a story to explain why there's two new men. He's got to change horses and be out of there in two minutes, so he won't have much time to think about it or ask questions. When he heads west from White Horse, he won't know it, but he'll be carrying a bunch of old useless paper, while we have the million dollars."

"When do you want us to leave for White Horse?" Joe asked.

"Us?"

"Me and Smiler."

"You're not going, Joe," Jessie said. "Smiler and Jack are handling the business at White Horse."

"Now hold on a minute," Joe said, "Jack here's just a boy."

"I'm almost eighteen, Pa," Jack protested.

Cherokee Joe frowned his son into silence.

"The two people running the operation at White Horse are a station keeper and a boy about Jack's age working as wrangler. That's the usual combination they keep in the smaller stations. We want everything to look as normal as possible when the rider from Salt Lake City comes in."

"All right, I can see that," Joe said. "But why Smiler? Why not me?"

"Because I've got other plans for you," Jessie said. "After we've got the money, I want us all to meet at a house I've got in Los Perros. That's just over the Mexican border at the Colorado River. It's not safe for a woman to ride down there alone, and I want you with me. We'll wait there together for Smiler and Jack to come with the greenbacks."

"I don't see why we got to go to all this infernal

trouble," Smiler said. "Why don't we just bring the loot back here and divvy it up?"

"Because it wouldn't do us a damn bit of good," Jessie said. "As soon as they open that mochila and find the greenbacks missing, every lawman between here and the Rockies will be looking for them. Maybe for us too by that time. If we're in Mexico the federal government can't touch us, and we can sit tight for as long as we have to."

"I ain't sure I'm followin' all this," Joe said. "If the U.S. government is goin' to be so all-fired anxious to get these greenbacks back, what earthly good are they gonna do us?"

"There are people in the South who will be happy to buy them from us. With gold. They won't pay the full million dollars, of course, but there will be plenty to make this worthwhile for all of us."

"What's the South gonna do with Federal greenbacks?" Smiler asked.

"Buy guns, for one thing. They got nobody down there building guns, and if they can pay with good greenbacks, there are plenty of gunmakers in the North who won't ask too many questions about where they came from."

"Ain't this bein' kinda disloyal to the Union?" Joe asked.

Jessie's eyes flashed in the lamplight. "What do you care? You're from Missouri. Anyway, what did the Union ever do for you besides lock you up?"

"I suppose that's true enough," Joe agreed.

"Miz McKee?"

Jessie looked over at the young man. "What is it, Jack?"

"I was wonderin', what happens to the Ace

Freighters after this? It's the onliest job I ever had and, well, I ain't sure I'm suited for anything else."

Jessie's voice grew more gentle. "I won't fool you, Jack, it looks like the company's going under. I've been fighting a losing battle for years trying to compete with Butterfield and the Central Overland. Now the telegraph's coming, so the mail contract won't mean a whole lot anyway. And when they get the railroad through it will be the end of the horse-drawn freight wagons. Our time is about up, Jack, but what we have here is a chance to get out of it all with enough money to live comfortably for the rest of our lives." She smiled at the others, her eyes glittering. "And when we go, we can ruin that sonofabitch Bill Russell at the same time."

Smiler and Cherokee Joe chuckled appreciatively. Jack did not join in, and Jessie regarded him thoughtfully.

"Is something bothering you, Jack?"

"Well, Miz McKee, to tell you the truth, I'm not real easy about what's gonna happen to them two men at the White Horse Pony station. The keeper and the wrangler. What I mean is, I don't think I could go along with killin' nobody who meant no harm to me."

Cherokee Joe frowned at his younger son. "Damn it, boy, it's time you started thinkin' like you was growed up. If you're choosin' to ride the owlhoot trail, you'd best know there's gonna be a dead man here and there along the way. If you can't stomach the thought, maybe you just ain't cut out for the life."

"It ain't that, Pa—" Jack began.

Jessie spoke up quickly. "It's all right, Jack. I'd just as soon avoid killing too, whenever it's possible. All that has to be done to the men at White Horse is tie them up and keep them out of the way long enough to switch the mochilas when the rider comes in. Isn't that right, Smiler?"

"Oh, sure, Jessie. We won't hurt nobody, less'n they force our hand." Smiler's tone was exaggeratedly casual, and Cherokee Joe gave him a quick look. Jack, however, seemed satisfied.

Jessie took a sheet of paper from her coat pocket, unfolded it and held it close to the lamp. "All right, here's the schedule. The greenbacks are due to leave St. Joe on Saturday, September first, at nine o'clock in the morning. That means the rider should reach White Horse Springs on Thursday at about noon. The Pony's been running within a few minutes of their schedule for the past couple of months, so we can expect them to be on time. When the rider comes into White Horse you, Smiler, and you, Jack will be waiting for him. Any questions so far?"

Smiler shook his head silently. He peered at Jack through squinted eyes.

"As soon as you've got the mochila with the greenbacks, you head for Los Perros. Do you know the town?"

"I know it," Smiler said. "It ain't a place I'd like to spend a whole lot of time."

"If things work out well we won't have to," Jessie said. "When you get there, Joe and I will be waiting." She refolded the mochila and passed it to Smiler.

"From now on we're going to be very careful about being seen together. Jack, you leave first and head back to town. Then Smiler and you, Joe, but don't ride together. I'll leave last."

"When do we get together next?" Smiler asked.

"I don't want to see you again, Smiler, until you ride into Los Perros with the money. You know when you've got to be at White Horse Springs. Make sure you and Jack leave on time."

"What about me?" Joe asked.

"You keep yourself available. I'll get hold of you when it's time for us to head south."

Jack stood up and looked around uncertainly. "Uh, how much time we got before we go, Smiler?"

"I'll let you know, boy," Smiler said. With a glance at Joe he added, "You just keep yourself available."

Jack nodded and turned to his father. "Well . . . so long for now, Pa."

Cherokee Joe stood up and walked out of the building with his son. "Adios, Jack." He put an unaccustomed hand on the boy's shoulder. "Don't worry, son. You're gonna do just fine."

"Thanks, Pa." The boy swung aboard his horse and was quickly lost in the shadows.

Cherokee Joe stood alone in the darkness listening to the diminishing hoofbeats. Then his skin prickled as he sensed someone standing behind him. He turned to see that Smiler had come silently out of the building. The exposed teeth glinted faintly where the puckered lip was pulled up.

"I hope your kid will pull his own weight on this trip," he said.

"Don't you worry none about Jack. You just keep hold of your own end of the rope."

"I'm used to doin' a man's work," Smiler said. "Have all my life. Not like some."

Cherokee Joe's eyes narrowed. "I ain't sure I catch your meanin', Smiler."

"I'll tell you this much, there ain't no woman gonna turn this child into no lap dog."

"I suspect you might be referrin' to me," Joe said.

"It does look like you been chose to stay with the womenfolk this trip."

Joe backed off a step and faced the other man. The clouds that had rolled in at dusk slid suddenly away from the moon, and the scene was lit with a pale, ghostly glow.

Joe said, "If you're gonna talk to a man like that, you better be ready to dig for iron."

Smiler held his hands well out in front of his body, keeping them plainly empty. "Uh-uh. You're faster'n me and I know it. I'd be a fool to slap leather with you."

"That's somethin' you shoulda thought about before you commenced runnin' off at the mouth."

Smiler spread his arms. "You wouldn't shoot a man with his hands empty."

Very deliberately Cherokee Joe eased the big old Walker Colt out of its holster and pointed it at the dead center of Smiler's chest. He thumbed the hammer back with a loud *klatch*.

Smiler's eyes widened as he stared at the mouth of the .44.

Joe spoke slowly and carefully. The gun never wavered. "Anybody who's been around as much as you ought to know better than to bet his life on what another man would do or wouldn't do. "

For another ten seconds he held the revolver rock steady. Droplets of sweat squeezed out of Smiler's forehead and glittered in the moonlight.

"Drop your gunbelt," Joe told him. "Do it real easy like."

While his eyes never left the muzzle of the Colt, Smiler carefully unbuckled his gunbelt and let it drop to the ground."

"That's the boy," Joe said. He eased the hammer

down and holstered his gun. He took off his own gunbelt then and laid it aside.

"Now, you crimp-lipped sonofabitch, you're gonna
get what you've been spoilin' for."

With a bellow, Cherokee Joe lowered his head and
charged, butting the other man at full speed in the
belly. All the air left Smiler in a great *whoosh,* and he
slammed to the ground on his back. Instantly Joe was
on top of him, pinning Smiler's arms with his knees.
He cared nothing for gentlemanly rules of combat, and
slammed his fists, one after the other, into Smiler's un-
protected face.

It took the sudden explosion of a gunshot close behind him to keep Cherokee Joe from beating Smiler to
death then and there. He turned to see Jessie McKee.
She stood gripping the big Walker Colt in both hands.

"Will you two misbegotten bastards stand up on
your feet and act like men?"

"He was askin' for it," Joe said.

Smiler mumbled something unintelligible through a
mouthful of blood.

"I don't want to hear about it," Jessie snapped. "Get
up on your feet or so help me, I'll blow the both of you
to Kingdom Come."

Joe hauled himself erect reluctantly. Smiler got to
his hands and knees and stayed in that position for a
minute retching and spitting blood. When he finally
stood up he wobbled like a drunk. His face was bloody
and starting to puff up.

Jessie tossed Joe's gun down on top of his belt. Both
men retrieved their weapons and buckled up.

"I want you two *cabròns* to stay clear of each other
until we've finished what we have to do," she said.
"After that I don't give a damn if you blow each

other's fool heads off. Meanwhile, I'm bankrolling this play, and don't either of you forget it."

Smiler found his hat, knocked the dirt off it, and settled it gingerly on his head. "I owe you for this, Cherokee," he said through battered lips, "and I aim to see that you get paid."

"Any time you're ready, you won't have far to look for me," Joe said.

Jessie smacked herself on the thigh with the flat of her hand. "Get the hell out of here, both of you. One at a time. I won't have your private quarrel messing up our chance at a killing."

Moving slow and stiff-legged, like a pair of fighting dogs, Smiler and Cherokee Joe mounted and rode off, taking separate trails back toward Sacramento. Jessie watched, frowning, until both were out of sight and she could no longer hear the hoofbeats of their horses. Then she walked slowly to her buggy.

24

It was a drizzly cold morning with a low cloud cover on the day Jack Bunker was supposed to ride out with Smiler. He stood beside his horse at the meeting place Smiler had selected outside Sacramento. Standing with him, looking more uncomfortable than the weather would account for, was Cherokee Joe.

"I won't hang around, son," Joe said, "since I got no wish to talk to Smiler. I just thought I'd ride out for a minute to, well, say so long and wish you luck."

"Thanks, Pa. I wish it was you I was ridin' out with today."

"So do I," said Joe. "But for this job you and me are just hired hands. We do what we're told. Afterward it'll be different. You and me'll be a team. How'd you like that?"

"I'd like it a lot." Jack looked around at the dripping trees and the scrub grass as though searching for something more to say.

Cherokee Joe coughed and spat on the ground. "I'd best be gettin' on back to town."

"I . . . I'm glad you come out, Pa," Jack said. "I mean it."

Cherokee Joe swung up into the saddle. He reached down and gripped Jack's hand. "A word of advice, son: don't turn your back on Smiler Tate."

"You think he'd do me dirt?"

"He'd steal from his mother if she gave him the chance. You'll be on the trail a long time with him. I'm just sayin' sleep with one eye open."

"I'll remember, Pa."

Cherokee Joe looked off up the road toward Sacramento. "Appears to be a buggy headin' this way. You weren't expectin' the Widow McKee out here, were you?"

"I sure wasn't." Puzzled, Jack peered through the misty rain at the approaching buggy. There was a woman at the reins, sure enough.

His father grinned suddenly. "Why, I do believe it's that purty young Beth Catlin come to say good-bye. You never told me there was somethin' goin' on betwixt you two."

"There ain't, Pa," Jack said earnestly.

"Just funnin' you, boy." Joe gave his son a thump on the shoulder. "Adiós, Jack. See you in Mexico."

"Good-bye, Pa." Jack watched as his father rode off up the road. Cherokee Joe touched his hat brim as he passed the oncoming buggy.

Jack caught the reins as Beth Catlin brought the buggy to a stop in the road where he stood. He gave her a hand, and she stepped down beside him. Her face was scrubbed pink. Little strands of pale blonde hair, damp from the mist, strayed out from under her bonnet. Jack thought he had never seen anything as beautiful.

"You'll get yourself all wetted down standin' out here," he said.

Beth gazed up at him. "I don't care. I just heard last

night from Mama that you were leaving and I made her tell me where you'd be. I couldn't let you go without saying good-bye."

"Now that's right thoughtful of you," Jack said. The words came with difficulty around a lump that had suddenly grown in his throat.

"Mama didn't say when you'd be coming back."

"I don't rightly know that myself," Jack told her. "I reckon that'll all be decided when your ma and the rest of us meet up in Los Perros."

"Los Perros? Where's that?"

"Beats me. Somewhere south of the border is all I know." Jack cocked his head and looked closely at the girl. "Does your ma know you come out here?"

"She knows, but she wasn't very happy about it," Beth said.

"I don't guess she would be."

Beth looked up earnestly into his eyes. "Jack, I want you to know that if things had been different . . . if I'd met you first . . . well . . ."

"You don't have to say it, Beth. Morgan always was better'n me at just about anything the both of us tried. When we was young'uns it didn't matter all that much. It seemed natural, him bein' older an' all. Thing is, Morgan kept on bein' just a mite better'n me even after we was growed. I always thought that someday I'd catch up to him, but so far it ain't happened."

Beth touched his cheek. "You mustn't feel that way. You're a different man than your brother. You'll find what you're meant to do one day, and you'll be better at it than Morgan or anybody else."

"I hope you're right," Jack said.

"I am. You'll see."

"So far I ain't been much of anything."

"You've been a good friend to me, Jack, and I want you to know I like you a lot."

"Well, that's somethin', I guess."

They stood in the mist for a moment of awkward silence. "Take care of yourself now, hear?" Beth said.

"Oh, I aim to."

"Well . . . good-bye then." Beth stood on tiptoe and kissed him quickly and lightly on the mouth.

It took Jack a moment to recover himself enough to help her back up into the buggy. "When you see my brother," he said, "tell him for me that he's a good man. But tell him that someday I'm gonna beat him at somethin'."

"I'll tell him," Beth said. She flicked the reins, wheeled the horse and buggy around, and headed back toward Sacramento.

Jack sat down on a fairly dry spot under a tree, hunched down into his coat, and thought about Beth Catlin and how her lips had felt in that one brief kiss. He was still thinking about her twenty minutes later when Smiler Tate rode up.

"What's the matter, boy, you sick or somethin'?" Smiler asked.

"Just thinkin'," Jack said.

"Well, mount up. You can think in the saddle. We got six days hard travelin' ahead of us to get to White Horse Springs."

Jack swung into the saddle, turned the sheepskin collar of his coat up around his ears, and fell in beside Smiler riding east.

Traveling with Smiler Tate turned out to be not very much fun. Smiler's answers to Jack's questions were limited to grunts and monosyllables. He complained frequently about having to wet nurse a boy along on a

they were up and saddled. They made a wide circle to the north and dropped back to the overland trail east of the relay station. Then they rode on into White Horse Springs trying their best to look like casual travelers.

The station keeper and the young wrangler came out to meet them. The keeper carried a Spencer carbine cradled in the crook of an elbow.

"Howdy, gents," he said. "Lose your way?"

"Howdy," Smiler said. "We're out huntin'."

The towheaded wrangler spoke up. "You'll find precious little to hunt on out the way you're headed."

"Less'n you got a taste for jackrabbit and prairie dog," the station keeper added, cackling.

"We heard there was antelope," Smiler said.

"Not around here," the keeper said. "You got to go all the way to the Wasatch to find antelope."

"I reckon we'll go on and try our luck anyway," Smiler said, "long as we come this far."

"Suit yourself. Like they say, there's plenty o' huntin' out there, but not much findin'." The man cackled again and slapped his thigh, raising a puff of dust.

"Mind if we water our horses?" Smiler asked.

"Shoot no, help yourself. There's a trough out back by the corral."

"I'll take 'em back for you," said the young wrangler.

Jack followed Smiler's lead and dismounted. He watched as the towhead led their horses back to the water, and felt a growing tightness high in his chest. The station keeper and the boy were being so downright friendly, Jack did not like to think about what was going to happen to them. At least he was glad they would not be seriously hurt.

"We don't get many travelers through here," the station keeper said.

"I reckon not," Smiler agreed, looking around at the desert landscape.

"My name's Kagle. The long-legged young'un is named Olson. We call him Ole."

"We're the Johnson brothers," Smiler said. "From Cheyenne. I'm Bob and this here's Bill."

"Pleased to meet you," Kagle said.

They shook hand all around. Jack started feeling sick.

When young Olson came back leading the horses Smiler signaled to Jack with his eyes to be ready. He sauntered over to take up a position where he and Jack could cover the men from both sides.

"You're welcome to take grub with us if you want," Kagle said. "We got ham and beans and corn bread aplenty."

"No thanks," Smiler said. He drew his six-shooters and covered the station keeper. "But I do believe we'll make use of your shack here for a little while."

Jack pulled his own guns and pointed them at Olson. The surprise and hurt in the young wrangler's eyes made him wish they could call the whole thing off.

"What the hell is this?" Kagle demanded. "Is this a joke?"

"If you think it's a joke," Smiler said, "try goin' for your gun. If you think we mean business, then grab yourself some sky."

Slowly the station keeper raised his hands. Jack motioned Olson over next to the older man with the barrel of his gun. He did not trust himself to speak.

"You're makin' a mistake," Kagle said. "We got nothin' here worth stealin'."

"Maybe not now, but you will in a little while. Get around to the back."

Kagle turned to Jack. "You, boy, what are you doin' ridin' with this coyote?"

"Shut up, old man," Smiler said, "if you want to see the sun come up again." To Jack he said, "Go inside and find some rope. And somethin' to stuff into their mouths so I don't hafta listen to any more of this old coot's yammerin'."

Avoiding the eyes of the station keeper and the young wrangler, Jack edged past them into the adobe hut. He quickly found a coil of stout rope, and pulled a blanket off one of the bunks that could be torn up and used as gags.

Back outside Smiler herded the two men around back to the toolshed. While Jack kept them covered, he worked swiftly and efficiently to gag and hogtie them both. With Jack's help, he shoved the bound men into the toolshed and latched the door. Jack wished he could talk to the men, assure them that they would not be harmed, but Smiler's expression warned him to keep his mouth shut.

They went back up front and unloaded the mochila they had brought with them stuffed with newspapers. They put it out of sight inside the station.

"Take our horses back over the rise there where they can't be seen from the trail," Smiler said.

Jack did as he was told, trying hard not to think about the two men locked in the cramped tool shed. When he came back he and Smiler saddled one of the two mustangs in the corral ready to go, and settled down to wait for the Pony Express rider.

Finally Jack had to say something. "You reckon those two are all right back there in the shed?"

"They might be a little bruised up, but they can take it for a couple of hours."

"Think they might need some water?"

"You just quit worryin' about them and keep your mind on what we come to do. You're supposed to be the wrangler here, so start actin' like one."

Jack went back to the corral and fed the mustangs a handful of grain each. It felt good to be with the horses, and away from Smiler. Still, the thought of the two men tied up in the shed plagued him. One a friendly old cuss who liked to talk and even offered to share his grub with them. The other a green boy Jack's own age or less. He made up his mind that once this was over he was finished with robbing folks. It was no way for a man to live.

A full hour ahead of schedule they heard the whoop of the incoming Pony rider. Jack led the saddled mustang around to the front of the station. Smiler stood by to make sure the rider didn't see anything he wasn't supposed to.

The rider, a wiry, dark-eyed boy, swung down to the ground as his lathered horse braced to a stop. He shot a curious look at Smiler and Jack.

"Where's Kagle and Ole?"

"They took sick sudden like," Smiler said. "Some kind of fever. They sent us out from Carson City to take over."

"Carson City? I don't remember you from there."

"We're new."

The rider looked as though he wanted to ask more questions, but precious seconds were slipping away. He trotted on out behind the station to relieve himself. Jack peeled the mochila from the rider's spent horse and tossed it into the station as Smiler brought out the one packed with newspapers. Jack took the new mochila and threw it across the saddle of the fresh mustang. When the rider came back, Jack had a dipper of cold water waiting for him. The rider drank thirstily, jumped into the saddle, and was off at a gallop in less than the alotted two minutes.

Jack and Smiler stood out in front of the station and watched him ride out of sight. When the dust had settled, Smiler went inside and brought out the mochila Jack had stashed there.

"I'm mighty curious about what a million dollars in greenbacks looks like," he said. With a Bowie knife he slashed one of the leather pouches and pulled out a packet wrapped in oiled silk. Inside the wrapper were thick bundles of freshly printed greenbacks.

Jack took one of the bundles and riffled the bills like a deck of cards. He studied the intricate face of the banknote.

"What's all this writin' say?" he asked.

"It don't matter," Smiler told him. "Only thing as counts is them numbers up in the corners. One-oh-oh-oh. That means each one of these little things is worth one thousand dollars."

Jack ran a finger across the printing on the bill. "I can't hardly believe people are gonna trade real gold for these fool things."

"That ain't for us to worry about," Smiler said. "Jessie McKee says she knows where she can turn these into real money. That's all I care about."

Smiler slashed open the other pouches and transfered the greenbacks to his own saddlebags. He rolled up the mochila and tossed it into the station.

"Go get the horses, boy," he said. "We got some hard ridin' to do."

Jack walked back and got their horses. He led them

back to the station, then stood holding them and looking at Smiler.

"Somethin' wrong, boy?"

"What about them two tied up in the shed?"

"What about 'em?"

"You ain't gonna just leave 'em there?"

Smiler snapped his fingers. "You're right, boy, we can't do that. I'm real glad you reminded me."

Smiler ambled around behind the station house while Jack stayed out front and busied himself with the packs and the horses. He was just as glad that he would not have to look into the eyes of the two men they had robbed again.

The crack of a pistol shot from out in back froze Jack where he stood.

A second shot echoed across the desert. Jack took off at a run toward the back of the station.

Smiler stood before the open door of the tool shed. In each hand was a smoking revolver. The bodies of Kagle and young Ole Olson, still bound, lay tumbled half in and half out of the shed. Beneath them was a spreading pool of blood.

"My Lord, what have you done?" Jack said.

Smiler turned slowly to face him. "Well now, like you said, we couldn't just leave 'em here. They could of told somebody what we look like. Now they can't."

"But . . . you killed 'em! Unarmed they was, and tied up to boot!"

"You know any better way to make sure they don't talk about us?"

"The Widow McKee said there weren't to be no killin'."

"The Widow McKee ain't the boss out here," Smiler said. "I am."

"You shouldn't of done it. I never agreed to go along with no killin'."

"Well, that's a shame, boy, because the killin's been done, and you're a part of it just as sure as if you'd pulled the trigger your own self."

"No I ain't," Jack said. "That was a dirty, cowardly thing to do, shoot them people whilst they was all tied up like that. I ain't no part of any of this with you no more, Smiler."

"Are you sure that's the way you want it?"

"You damn right I'm sure." At that moment Jack Bunker knew in his heart that he was at last truly a man.

"All right, boy," Smiler said in a voice soft as a snake's hiss. He swung one of the guns around and fired.

The slug hit Jack in the middle of the chest with the force of a sledgehammer. He sat down hard, more surprised than hurt for a second. He tried to get at his own gun, but his hands wouldn't move the way he wanted them to. He coughed once and his mouth filled with blood. Then the pain hit him in the chest like a red-hot branding iron.

"Let that be a lesson to you, boy," said Smiler from the end of a long tunnel. "Don't never feel sorry for nobody." He turned and walked away toward the horses.

Jack watched through a red-flecked haze of pain as Smiler mounted up and rode off without another backward look. Then big chunks of the world fell away and everything was black and there was a great rushing in his ears . . .

And then there was nothing.

26

WHEN Morgan Bunker galloped out of Placerville bound for Sacramento, carrying the mochila that was supposed to contain the greenbacks, nine days had passed since the shipment left St. Joseph. And four days had passed since his brother and two employees of the Pony Express had died at White Horse Springs. The riders had carried along the report of the sudden illness of the station keeper and wrangler at White Horse, but the later news of the killings was, naturally, behind them. Still, a sense of impending trouble lurked in the back of Morgan's mind as he urged the mustang on to cover the last 50 miles of the run.

By that time, the middle of September, the arrival of the Pony rider in Sacramento was no longer the big event it had been at the beginning. Out on the vast stretches of open space in the west, it was still an exciting occasion to see the rider gallop past, but in the bigger cities along the way it had become routine.

There was, however, a special reception committee on hand for this ride of Morgan Bunker's, because of the shipment he was thought to be carrying. An official of the U.S. Treasury was there, the Postmaster of Sacramento, and a representative of the Governor of California. Also present, and more nervous than the rest, was William Russell of the Central Overland. The calmest man on the scene, as usual, was Bolivar Roberts.

When Morgan rode in, Roberts was outside to greet him. The superintendent shook Morgan's hand when the young rider dismounted, and pulled the mochila from the mustang's back himself.

"Any problems?" Roberts asked.

"Nope. Everything smooth as glass."

The man from the Treasury came out and took personal charge of the mochila. Morgan watched curiously.

"Who's that?"

"Government man from Washington," Roberts said.

"Uh-huh. Mr. Roberts, can I ask you something?"

"Ask away, son."

"I know I was carryin' something special this time in the mochila. We all did. Can you tell me now what the heck it was?"

"I reckon the need for secrecy is past now," Roberts said. "What you had in the four lock boxes on that mochila was U.S. greenbacks. One million dollars' worth."

"Greenbacks? What on earth for?"

"I'm afraid I can't give you a very good answer to that one," Roberts said, "mostly because I don't truly understand it myself. I know it has something to do with keeping California on the side of the Union if the Southern states do go ahead and secede like they're threatening to."

"What has a million dollars in paper money got do do with that?" Morgan asked.

"Son, it beats me."

Inside the office the Treasury man, the Postmaster, and the governor's representative stood around the counter as William Russell inserted a tiny flat key in the lock of the first mail pouch. His hand trembled.

The key refused to turn in the lock.

"What's wrong?" asked the Treasury man.

"I can't get this fool key to work."

"Here, let me try."

The Treasury man twisted the key back and forth with no success.

William Russell began to perspire.

"Could it be the wrong key?" asked the Postmaster.

"I don't see how. Let me try it again." Russell took the key back and worked it into the second of the lock boxes. No results. He tried the third, then the fourth and last. By this time he was sweating heavily. "It *must* be the wrong key."

While the others exchanged worried glances, Russell stepped to the door of the office and opened it. "Mr. Roberts, will you come in here a minute?"

The superintendent excused himself from Morgan and went inside. "What is it, Mr. Russell?"

William Russell's voice had gone suddenly hoarse. "I can't get the damn mail pouches unlocked. Could you have given me the wrong key?"

"Let me see it."

Russell handed over the key. Roberts held it up to the light and squinted at the tiny number that was stamped into the metal. "This is the right key," he said.

"Then why the devil won't it work?"

Roberts walked over to the counter where the mochila lay surrounded by the four worried-looking men. He bent down and examined the lock on one of the four pouches. After a moment he straightened up and faced William Russell. "The numbers don't match. This is the right key, but that's the wrong mochila."

"What? Are you sure?"

"Check the numbers for yourself."

"No, no, I'll take your word for it, but how could such a thing have happened?"

"I can't say, but I suggest that before we do anything else we open these pouches and see what's inside."

"Quite right, quite right," Russell agreed, pulling out a handkerchief to mop his forehead.

"Do you have a key here that will work?" the Postmaster asked.

"Probably," Roberts said, "but I'd rather not take the time to hunt it up."

He drew a hunting knife from a sheath on his belt and touched the tip of the blade to the mochila. To William Russell he said, "With your permission, sir?"

"Yes, yes, go ahead," Russell said. He ran a finger down inside his stiff collar.

While the others leaned forward like medical students watching a master surgeon cut into a patient, Bolivar Roberts inserted the knife point and deftly sliced through the stout leather of one of the four mail pouches. He reached in through the opening and drew out the package inside. His eyes met those of William Russell as they saw that the package was wrapped not in the usual oiled silk, but in plain brown paper.

Not a sound could be heard in the room as Roberts cut the twine that bound it and unwrapped the brown paper from the package. As one, the four men gasped.

William Russell reached out and seized the contents of the package in both hands. "Newspapers!" he cried. "Cut up newspapers!"

"What is the meaning of this?" the man from the Treasury demanded.

"Where is the money?" cried the Postmaster.

"How the hell would I know?" Russell sputtered.

The man from the governor's office stood by silently looking miserable.

Russell faced Bolivar Roberts. "What about this? Do you have an explanation?"

"Let's all calm down for a minute," said Roberts, "and see if we can figure it out. First of all, we know the greenbacks were packed in the mochila when it left St. Joe."

"Of course we do," Russell said impatiently. "What I want to know is where are they now?"

"That's what we all want to know, Mr. Russell," Roberts said quietly. "Now, standard procedure is to check the contents of the mochila in Fort Laramie and again in Salt Lake City."

"That's right," the treasury agent verified. "We had agents at both locations this time to verify that the money was all there."

"Somewhere between Salt Lake City and Sacramento," Roberts continued, "this mochila was substituted for the one that carried the greenbacks. The different numbers on the locks and on the key tells us that."

"I just don't see how it's possible," Russell said.

"How trustworthy are your riders?" asked the Postmaster. "The ones who carried the mail between Salt Lake City and here?"

Bolivar Roberts stiffened. "I will personally vouch for each and every one of them."

"I'll back him up on that," William Russell agreed. "All of our riders are hand-picked men. There has never been a suggestion of dishonesty among them." He frowned thoughtfully and spoke to Roberts. "Still, we'll want to talk to each of the men who carried the mochila west of Salt Lake City."

"I'll arrange it," Roberts said.

"One of them could have information that would tell us where and how the mochila was switched. Suppose we start right now with the young man who just rode in. Bunker, isn't it?"

Roberts nodded. "Morgan Bunker. He's one of our very best."

"Ask him to come in, will you?"

"If I may, sir, I'd like a few minutes to talk to him alone first."

"Oh, very well." William Russell eased himself into a chair. "But don't keep us waiting too long."

Morgan stood with his mouth open when Bolivar Roberts told him the news. In the five months of its operation there had never been a hint of tampering with the Pony Express mail. It always came through intact. Once a rider had ridden his pony to exhaustion, but when the animal could go no farther the boy had run the seven miles to the next station carrying the heavy mochila. On another occasion the rider had fallen and hurt himself badly, but the pony carried the mochila in safely. Although a rider or a horse might have gone down, the mail always went through.

"I can't believe it, Mr. Roberts," Morgan said when he found his voice.

"I know how you feel, son, but somehow, somewhere that mochila was switched."

"But how? Where?"

"Think hard. Did anything unusual happen on your run? At Placerville? Any of the relay stations?"

"Nothin'," Morgan said. "Everybody was lookin' sharp cause they knew there was somethin' special about this run."

"There weren't any strangers hanging around the stations? Or on the trail?"

"Not that I saw."

Roberts' big shoulders rose and fell in a heavy sigh.

"I wish I could help you," Morgan said, "but I just can't think of anything that was any different on this run."

"That's all right, son," Roberts said. "There are some men inside now who want to talk to you. They're all pretty upset about losing the money, but don't let them rattle you. Just answer their questions the best you can."

"Yes, sir. And after I'm through in there?"

"I think you'd better stay in Sacramento for a few days. I'll arrange a room for you."

Morgan started to go into the office, then hesitated. "Mr. Roberts, tell me somethin'."

"Sure, son."

"Does anybody think I had somethin' to do with stealin' that money?"

"No, Morgan, nobody's accusing anybody yet. But I'll tell you this, until we find out what happened to that million dollars, the whole Pony Express is under suspicion. And that includes everybody from Mr. William Russell down to the greenest wrangler. So you just tell those men inside what you know, then stand by till you hear from me."

Morgan nodded, squared his shoulders, and walked into the office.

27

MORGAN spent the night in a room in a boarding house that Bolivar Roberts found for him. He did not sleep much. The session in the Pony Express office answering questions for Mr. Russell and the others had left him jumpy and out of sorts. Mr. Russell himself had been kindly enough, but the other men were excitable, and their questions got downright insulting some of the time.

He understood that losing a million dollars, even though it was just paper money, would be worrisome to the Treasury man and the Postmaster. What he did not like was the way they suggested that one of the Pony riders might have something to do with it.

After Bolivar Roberts left him at the boarding house, Morgan had gone around looking for his father and his brother. When he couldn't find them, it was one more worry to keep him awake. He had not realized how much he counted on their support in time of trouble. Even the Widow McKee, who might have had some word of Jack and Cherokee Joe, was gone without leaving word where she was going. Morgan found it all mighty peculiar.

The next day he was up early to try again, but did not do any better. He tried all the saloons where he knew his father hung out, but nobody had seen Cherokee Joe for several days. Never in his life had Morgan felt so alone.

That afternoon he was sitting dejectedly on his bed, staring out the window at nothing, when Bolivar Roberts came in. The big man's expression was grim.

"Is somethin' wrong, Mr. Roberts?" he asked.

"I'm afraid so, son," said the superintendent. "I wish it wasn't up to me to do it, but I've got to give you some mighty bad news. I guess there's no way to do it but to just tell you straight out. Morgan, your brother's dead."

For a moment the words did not register on Morgan. His brother Jack was only seventeen, and healthy as a draft horse.

"There must be a mistake," he said.

"No mistake," Roberts said, and Morgan knew in his heart that it was true.

"How'd it happen?"

"He was shot. It happened at the White Horse Springs relay station just out of Salt Lake City."

"Where'd you hear about it?"

"A rider just came in with the news. The station keeper at White Horse and the wrangler were shot too. They're all dead."

"I don't follow all this. What was Jack doin' all the way back in White Horse Springs?"

"From the looks of things," Roberts said, "he was there to steal the shipment of greenbacks."

"I just can't believe that," Morgan said.

"I know, son. I met your brother, and it's hard for me to believe too, but there was a witness."

"Somebody saw him?"

"The wrangler there, a boy named Olson, was still alive when they found him, but just barely. He said Jack and an older man tied them up and locked them in the tool shed the morning the rider was due in with the greenbacks. They gave the rider that story about the station keeper and Olson coming down sick, then switched the mochila when they got a chance."

"Who was it shot Jack?" Morgan asked.

"Olson died before he could give any more details. As near as we can piece it together, either him or the station keeper must have got off a shot and hit Jack before they were gunned down. There was nobody else around who could have done it."

"What happened to the man who was supposed to be with Jack?"

"He got away. Took the money with him."

Morgan hesitated before asking the next question. "Have they got any idea who the man is?"

Bolivar Roberts walked over and stared out the window for a moment, then turned around. "Morgan, do you know where your father is?"

"Pa? You're not thinkin' my Pa had anything to do with this?"

"I'm trying not to think anything, but you've got to admit it doesn't look too good. We all know Cherokee Joe Bunker's reputation.

"That's all behind him now," Morgan said.

"Maybe, but there's a lot of people going to say once an outlaw, always an outlaw. And then there's the fact that your brother was on the scene."

"Jack never broke no law in his life. Leastwise, no important law."

"He's Cherokee Joe's son," Roberts said,

"So am I," Morgan answered.

Roberts sighed unhappily. "I know you are, Morgan. And speaking for myself, I'd trust you any time, any place. But since I don't know your father and your brother as well as I know you, I can't say the same for them."

Morgan stared at him. "Are you tellin' me that people are gonna think that my Pa, my brother, and me was all in on it together? The Bunker gang?"

"I'm afraid that's the way some people are going to think."

"That just beats all."

"I agree, but there's nothing I can do about it," Roberts said. "There'll be some Federal officers coming around who'll want to talk to you, so you better stick close by."

Morgan walked over to the door and opened it. "Mr. Roberts, I want you to know I appreciate that it was you who come to tell me this."

"I wish there was more I could do," Roberts said. "Is there a message I can pass on to anybody for you?"

"It don't seem so. Everybody I know out here is either out of town or . . . or dead." Morgan's voice went husky, and he covered it with a cough. Bolivar Roberts looked away and appeared not to notice.

"You can find me any time at the Central Overland office," he said. "If I'm not there, somebody will go and fetch me."

"I'll remember," Morgan said.

Roberts hesitated, as though searching for some way to say goodbye, then decided to say nothing at all. He went out the door and Morgan closed it behind him.

28

AFTER Bolivar Roberts left him alone in the room, Morgan felt all cold and numb. It was something like the time back on Uncle Henry's farm when a mule kicked him in the back. He was only ten years old at the time, but he never forgot the sensation of lying there and looking down at his body as though it belonged to somebody else since he couldn't feel anything. However, this time it was different. There was a core of icy pain growing inside him that would have to come out sooner or later, but for now he kept it locked in.

Jack was dead. The words sounded all wrong. It was near impossible for Morgan to picture his lively, ornery, eager younger brother lying all dead and still. In his eighteen years Morgan had seen dead men enough, but Jack did not belong with them. It all had to be some terrible mistake. And yet he knew there was no mistake. Bolivar Roberts would not come in here and tell him his brother was dead unless he was damn well sure it was true.

And now his father too. What had become of Cherokee Joe? Over the last couple of years Morgan had watched the old man grow restive as a nominal employee of Ace Freighters, without any real job to do except service the Widow McKee. It had worried him that Joe might return to his outlaw ways one day. And knowing how Jack worshiped the old man, it had also occurred to Morgan that his younger brother might follow him. But he never imagined it could end like this, his brother shot dead and his father on the run, wanted for robbing the very company Morgan worked for.

Morgan sat down heavily on the bed. The story did not fit. There was no denying Cherokee Joe had his faults, more than his rightful share. And it was even possible he would rob the company his eldest son worked for. But he would never run off and leave his own boy lying dead for the buzzards.

Morgan smacked a fist into his hand. He could not believe that of his father. He *would* not believe it. It gave him one thought he could cling to in his world that had suddenly turned all upside down.

A soft rapping at the door pulled Morgan away from his thoughts. He walked across to open it.

Beth Catlin stood out in the hall. She said, "Hello, Morgan."

He stood for a long moment just looking at her, unable to speak. She had on a new bonnet and a soft-looking dress of cornflower blue that matched her eyes. Standing there she looked pretty enough to make a man cry. In fact, Morgan was shocked to realize, he *was* crying.

Just as though it were the most natural thing in the world, Beth came into his arms. She hugged him tight and pulled his head down so his flushed cheek lay against her cool one. Morgan's shoulders heaved as he fought to hold back the sobs that were building up in his chest.

"Go ahead, Morgan, let go," she said softly. "The strongest men in the world have got to cry sometimes. Mr. Roberts told me where you were. He told me about Jack too. I thought you'd want to be with someone."

Morgan tried to answer her, but when he opened his mouth it was not words that came out, it was the pain he had held inside for so many hours. He cried as he had not done since his mother died. Beth held him and stroked his hair and murmured little loving words. And for a time the 16-year-old girl was a woman wise as the earth, and the 18-year-old man was a child.

Somehow—Morgan could never remember how it happened—they were both lying on the bed. Morgan held the girl to him with all his strength, and she responded with her entire body. Ever so gradually his sobs diminished and finally stopped. Still he kept his arms around her. He became aware all at once that he was getting excited. With Beth lying right up against him the way she was, she could not fail to notice. Abruptly, he was ashamed of himself and tried to draw away from her.

Beth continued to hold him. "Don't," she whispered. "I don't want you to stop."

"But . . . but I—"

"Hush now," she said. "I know all about men and men's needs. Nobody talks about it, but us women have our needs too. When the time is right, and the two people are right for each other, then they ought to be together. Really together."

"But you ain't never . . . done it? Have you?"

Beth raised her head and looked into his eyes. She

smiled gently. "No, I never did it with any man before. I never wanted to. But now I do. With you."

In spite of trying to hold it down, Morgan found himself growing more excited with every beat of his heart. "I couldn't," he said. "Not with you, Beth."

"Why not? You love me, don't you?"

"I . . . how the heck would I know?"

"If you love somebody, you know," she said with an edge to her voice.

"All right, dang it, I love you," Morgan got out. "I ain't never said that before, and it ain't easy."

She rewarded him with a beautiful smile. "I love you too, Morgan. That's why anything we do together is all right, you see, as long as we do it with love."

It was a brand new idea to Morgan, one he could not readily get a handle on. The way he had always figured, you either did it with loose women like the Pryor sisters, or you did it with a whore. Then when you got married, you did it with your wife, but that was different. Of course, in some cases it was all right to do it with the woman who would become your wife. Morgan seized on the last thought, and it suddenly seemed all right. When he took a wife, he could not imagine it being anyone other than Beth Catlin.

"I really do love you, Beth," he said.

"There, you see how it makes everything all right?"

Then he was kissing her. Her lips were unbelievably soft, and seemed to mold themselves to his mouth. He inhaled the clean lilac-soap smell of her and tasted the sweetness of her tongue.

Beth worked an arm in between them and unbuttoned the top of her dress. She pulled it down off her shoulders to expose her round, high-standing breasts. Their skin was transluscent, like pearls. The nipples were a rosy red-brown. Morgan could not take his eyes off them.

She took his hand and placed it over one of her breasts. He felt the small nipple grow erect under his palm. He held her as he would some delicate bird.

"Squeeze me," she whispered. "Go ahead. You won't hurt me."

He did as she asked. The firm flesh of her breast yielded under his fingers. The sensation drove him wild with wanting her. He dropped his head and kissed her breast. The nipple slipped into his mouth. He sucked it gently. Beth moaned softly and stroked the back of his head. He would never have believed that a woman could taste so good.

"Wait a minute," she whispered.

Breathing hard, Morgan pulled away and looked at her curiously. For a frightening moment he thought she was going to jump up and run out of the room, grossly insulted, never to return. She gave him a smile that put his fears to rest. Flecks of fire glowed deep in her cornflower eyes.

"Close your eyes now," she told him.

"What?"

"Go on, close your eyes. I'm not used to having a man watch me undress."

Morgan swallowed hard and closed his eyes. His heart was beating so hard he fancied it could be heard all over the room. He listened to her moving lightly about. There was the rustle of cloth, the gentle scrape of a chair on the floor, a pad of bare feet, then the bed sagged next to him. He felt the comforter pulled up to cover the both of them.

Beth said, "You can open your eyes now."

Her head was on the pillow close to his. The blonde hair was loose and tumbled. She was smiling. He reached out tentatively and felt the smooth, warm skin of her body. He kissed her lips.

After a minute he said, "Now you got to close your eyes."

"Really? I didn't think men worried about things like that."

"Fair's fair."

"Oh, all right." Playfully Beth pulled the comforter up over her head. Morgan scrambled out of bed and pulled off his clothes hastily. He was glad he had stopped at the barber shop this morning for a shave and a bath. He turned the lamp down so there was only a soft glow in the room, and started back to bed. Then he saw Beth sitting up, watching him.

He jumped back into bed and snatched the comforter over himself. "You looked."

"Mm-hmm. Are you mad at me?"

"I oughta be. You cheated."

"But *are* you?"

A big foolish grin spread over his face. "I don't think I could ever really be mad at you."

"Maybe I'll remind you of that someday," she said. "But we can talk about that later." She moved close to him so their naked bodies were touching all along their length.

Morgan said, "Beth, are you sure . . . I mean, do you really want to . . ."

"Of course I want to, you darn fool. Why else would I be here naked as a jaybird in your bed? But if you don't quit talking about it, I might get out of the notion."

Morgan quit talking about it then and there. He kissed Beth Catlin and he caressed her and he made love to her in ways he had only imagined.

He was very gentle at first, almost hesitant, afraid of

hurting her. When the barrier broke she gave a little cry, then clasped him against her more tightly than ever. She thrust her body against him, taking him inside her with a wild kind of joy.

For Morgan the climax came not suddenly and explosively as it had with the Pryor sisters, but in a sweet, lingering moment of joy that was so intense it was almost painful. They cried out together with one voice and clung to each other as though to save themselves from drowning.

Gradually, softly, the passion subsided. They lay quietly side by side, his hand clasping hers, her leg thrown comfortably over his. As their breathing returned to near normal Morgan rolled his head to look at her. He was fearful that he might see something in her eyes that he did not want to. Disappointment. Or worse, disgust. He went weak with relief when Beth looked back at him with eyes that brimmed with love.

"It was beautiful, Morgan," she said, sensing his concern. "Just beautiful."

He squeezed her hand. "I never knowed that a girl . . . a woman enjoyed it too."

"You'd be surprised to know some of the things a woman feels."

"I expect I would, at that."

They lay comfortably together for many minutes without speaking. Beth rolled onto her side and propped her head up, the better to look at him. With gentle fingers she smoothed away a frown line between his brows.

"What are you thinking about?" she asked.

"Nothin' I ought to burden you with. Not at a time like this."

"What do you mean not at a time like this? Now more than ever I'm entitled to know about you. I want to know what pleases you and what hurts you. What makes you happy, and what things do you worry about. We're more like one person now, Morgan."

"That's true," he admitted. "I guess I was thinkin' about my brother Jack. We ain't seen a whole lot of one another in the last couple of years, but I'm gonna miss him."

"Of course you are. Jack thought an awful lot of you too."

"It's just such a dang shame he had to go the way he did," Morgan said. "He had no schoolin' to speak of, but he was a smart, hard-workin' lad, and he mighta made somethin' of himself."

Beth snuggled close to him, her hand resting on his bare chest, listening. The warmth and vitality of her young body against his gave Morgan strength, encouraged him to talk about things he had never put into words before.

"Sometimes I think I didn't do all I should have to steer Jack down the right road. I was the older brother. It was up to me to take care of him."

"You did what you could," Beth said. "You tried to get him a job riding for the Pony Express."

"That I did," Morgan said. "Might have done it too, if it hadn't been for Pa."

He stopped talking, and frowned.

"What is it?" Beth asked.

"I was thinkin' about our Pa. It just ain't like him to ride off and leave Jack lyin' out there on the desert with a bullet in him.

"But he didn't," Beth said. "Your father wasn't with Jack."

Morgan sat straight up in bed. "He wasn't?"

"No. I talked to Jack the morning he rode out. He was going with the man called Smiler."

Morgan slapped the bed beside him. "I mighta knowed!"

"I'm not saying he wasn't involved in the robbery. I think they were all in it—your father, my mother, Jack and Smiler. But your father didn't have anything to do with the shooting out there at White Horse Springs. He and my mother headed south together. I think they all planned to meet later."

Morgan seized her arm. "Do you know where they were going, your Ma and my Pa?"

"I'm not sure. Some place in Mexico. Jack mentioned the name before he left."

"What is it? What's the name?"

"I'm trying to think."

"Think hard, Beth. It could be mighty important."

She looked off up into the corner of the room, as though she might spy the name etched into the ceiling there.

"Please, honey," Morgan urged.

"Los something. Let me see. I remember, it was Los Perros."

"Los Perros," he repeated. "Are you sure?"

"Yes, that was it. I've heard my mother talk about it before. I think my father had some kind of business dealing down there."

"Los Perros," Morgan said softly, almost to himself.

"What are you going to do?"

"I'm going down there."

"But why?"

"I've got a number of reasons," he said. "First I want to see my Pa and tell him what happened to Jack before that Smiler fills him full of lies. Also, there's a million dollars' worth of greenbacks floatin' around somewhere that belongs to the Pony Express. And most important, I can face down the man who left my brother lyin' in the desert with a bullet in him."

"You'd go up against Smiler?"

"In a minute."

"He's killed men, Morgan."

"So have a lot of fellers."

"Will you kill him?"

"If I have to."

Beth pulled the comforter up tight under her chin. "Morgan, when it's over, will you come back to me?"

He rolled over to look at her. The scowl faded. "Beth honey, as long as I can ride, walk, or crawl along the ground, I'll come back to you. That's a promise."

They embraced and held onto each other tightly, a little desperately, as though they were already being pulled apart by forces they could not control.

29

LATE September in the deep Southwest can be the hottest time of the year. It is not a time that is pleasant for travelers. Jessie McKee and Cherokee Joe Bunker learned this painfully as the sun blazed down on them without let-up all the way from Sacramento to the border east of Mexicali where they rode across into Mexico.

They had ridden hard for ten days, and neither of them felt much like talking as they crossed the dry, treeless landscape.

When they had started out from Sacramento in the cool dawn there had been a good deal of laughter and joshing between them. But spending twelve and fourteen hours a day in the saddle had soured their spirits as well as bruised their bodies. It further rankled Joe that the woman seemed to be bearing up as well as he was. At first he had laughed at Jessie's insistence on riding astraddle her horse like a man, but he soon saw that she would never have made it trying to hold the awkward side-saddle seat that was expected of ladies.

As the sun reached its midday height Joe pulled off

his grimy bandana and mopped the sweat from his eyes.

"Are you sure there really is a Los Perros?" he said. "It don't look to me like there's nothin' but desert between here and the Gulf of Mexico."

"The town is there," Jessie assured him.

"Then I hope we're headin' the right way. It'd be a damn shame if we missed the fool place."

"We're going the right way," Jessie said. "Why don't you leave off bellyaching for a while?"

Joe lapsed into a sullen silence as they rode on over the arid land. He longed for the lush prairies and cool forests of Missouri. If he had known where she was leading him, he would have damn well told her to find herself somebody else. This was not his idea of the way a man ought to live.

After another hour they came to a range of low, rounded hills. As they reached the crest of one of these, a sort of dished-out valley lay before them. A stream meandered through, providing a strip of green in the monotonous brown land. On the near bank was a cluster of small square buildings of sun-bleached adobe with a dusty street running down the center. The street came to a sudden end at a house slightly larger than the rest, which backed up to a hill to the north.

Joe glowered down at the little settlement. "It sure ain't no Garden of Eden."

"I didn't pick the place for its beauty," Jessie said. "I picked it because it's a good place to hide."

"That's a fact," Joe agreed. "It ain't likely a feller would happen on it accidental."

They rode down toward the village in silence for several minutes. Then Jessie said, "Where did you hear about the Garden of Eden?"

"I learned a thing or two from the Good Book when I was a boy. I ain't completely ignorant, you know."

"I know that, Joe. I didn't mean it to sound that way."

Her voice was suddenly so gentle that Joe swung around in the saddle to look at her. She smiled at him. He couldn't help but grin back at her, and suddenly he started feeling a good deal better.

They rode together into the sun-baked town of Los Perros. The Mexican villagers stood silently on both sides of the street watching them impassively.

"I don't like the looks of these people," Joe said. "They'd as soon stick a knife 'twixt our ribs as spit."

"Don't be so damn suspicious," Jessie told him. She pulled off the slouch hat she wore for protection from the sun and shook out her thick coppery hair.

The villagers brightened immediately.

"*La Roja!*" they cried. "*La Roja volve!*"

Joe's hand moved for his gun. "What are they sayin'?" he asked out of the side of his mouth.

"It means Redhead. That's what they call me here."

"These bean-eaters know you?"

"Sure. I told you I had a house down here. Jim McKee built it before he died while he was trying to work some deal for Mexican silver. It never came to anything, but I kept the house and spread enough pesos around so the people would remember me."

She pulled up before a group of the Mexicans and spoke in slow, precise Spanish. They smiled and nodded and pointed toward the adobe at the end of the street.

"You never told me you talked the lingo," Joe said.

"You never asked me."

"What did you say to them?"

"I asked if my house was ready."

"And is it?"

"Oh, sure. They tell me there's been a family living in it, just to watch over the place and keep it clean for me."

"I'll bet."

"They say I am welcome, and so is my friend, *El Furioso.*"

"Who's that?"

Jessie smiled mischievously. "That's you. Roughly, it means the angry one."

"Angry one, eh? Well, what the hell do they expect? I been in the saddle more'n a week without a decent meal, a proper drink, or as much as a kind word. Hell, who wouldn't be *furioso*?"

A boy of about twelve stepped forward and spoke shyly to Jessie.

"This is Roberto," Jessie said. "He says he'll water the horses for us."

"Why?"

"He's just being friendly. Come on, that's the house at the end of the street. We can walk from here."

They dismounted, and the boy led the horses down toward the stream.

"We'll be lucky to ever see them animals again," Joe grumbled.

"Don't be such a grouch. These people only want to help us."

"Uh-huh." Joe scowled around at the smiling group of villagers that accompanied them to the house at the end of the street.

As they approached, a family that seemed to include at least twenty members of three generations spilled out and lined the path to the door, smiling and chattering in Spanish.

Jessie nodded and smiled back at them and kept saying, *"Gracias, gracias."*

"Who are all these chili peppers?" Joe asked.

"It's the family who've been taking care of my house. Their name is Gonzales."

"Down here everybody's name is Gonzales."

"They say they will be happy to serve us in any way they can."

"They can serve me by going away," Joe grumbled.

The Gonzales family looked at him curiously. Jessie spoke to them in her careful Spanish. The brown faces creased into expressions of kindly concern. They shook their heads and made sympathetic noises at Joe.

"What did you say to them?" he demanded.

Jessie batted her eyelashes at him. "I told them that you were really a nice man, but you had saddle boils so bad it hurt you to smile."

"You got half of it right, anyhow."

"Are you ready to take a look at our house, *El Furioso*?"

"Lead the way, Redhead."

They went inside and found the one large room blessedly cool, insulated by the thick adobe walls and roof. There was a big open hearth on one wall, with cooking utensils hanging from pegs. There was a broad wooden table, several chairs, a chiffonier with no legs and, to Joe's amazement, a sturdy brass double bed.

"Where in tarnation did that come from?" he said.

"I had it carted in after the last time McKee and me had to sleep on the floor. I figured if I had occasion to be here again, I would damn well sleep comfortable."

Joe wrapped an arm around her waist and started toward the bed. "What are we waiting for? Tell the Gonzales family to vamoose and we'll try it out."

"Not so fast," Jessie said. "Before I do anything

else, and I mean *anything*, I'm going to have me a bath."

"I swear, you are the most bath-minded woman I ever knowed."

Jessie turned to the smiling Gonzaleses. *"Quiero baño,"* she said.

They kept smiling and nodding, but their faces showed no understanding.

"Baño, baño," Jessie said, repeating the word very slowly.

Still no response.

" 'Pears they ain't all that familiar with baths down here," Joe said, chuckling.

"Never mind," Jessie said. She tried again with the Mexicans. *"Hay agua caliente? Jabón?"* She made washing motions with her hands, as though soaping her body. She scowled at Cherokee Joe, who was enjoying the performance hugely. *"Deseo lavarse."*

The face of one of the young Gonzales girls brightened. She whispered something into the ear of the well-padded Mamacity, who seemed to be leader of the clan. The woman beamed in sudden comprehension.

"Ah, sí, Senora!" She rattled off orders in Spanish to several of the children and sent them scurrying off toward the village. *"Agua caliente,"* she said proudly to Jessie, *"Y jabón."*

"Gracias," Jessie said, smiling happily. *"Muchas gracias."*

Cherokee Joe, grinning, started to settle into a chair. "This ought to be interestin'."

Jessie caught hold of his arm and pulled him back up. "If you think you're going to hang around and watch me take a bath, you're crazy."

"Well, where d'you expect me to go?"

"There's a cantina in the village. That ought to keep you entertained for an hour or so."

"What cantina? I didn't see anything that looked like a saloon when we rode in."

"Come on, I'll point it out to you."

They walked together to the head of the street. Abruptly Joe seized Jessie's arm while he pulled his gun.

"What the hell are you doing?" she said.

He nodded toward a clump of prickly pear about six feet ahead of them. A diamondback rattlesnake, thick around as a man's forearm, lay coiled in the shadow of the cactus.

"Rattler," Joe said.

"What about it?"

"I'm fixin' to shoot the varmint, that's what about it."

"Why?"

"Because he's a rattler, for cryin' out loud. What more reason do you need?"

"This is the desert, Joe. You can't kill all the snakes that live out here."

"I can sure as hell kill me this one." Joe cocked the revolver and took aim.

Jessie held his arm. "Can't you let him be? He's not hurting anybody, just having himself a nap in the shade."

Joe stared at her. "Sometimes I don't understand you, woman. It's nothin' but a durn snake."

"I just don't like to kill anything unless it's necessary. We can walk around him easy enough."

Joe heaved a big sigh. He uncocked the Colt and dropped it back into the holster. "All right, Jessie, I'll let your fool snake live, but I'm durned if I know why I'm doin' it."

Jessie gave his arm a squeeze. "You're doing it to make me happy."

Joe spat into the dust to cover his embarassment.

"There's the cantina," Jessie said, pointing, "the last building at the end of the street."

"Enjoy your bath," he said. "I'll see you later."

He left her walking back to the house and ambled down the dusty street toward the cantina. Halfway there he met a group of laughing Gonzaleses carrying a huge iron cauldron back the other way. He scowled at them. They answered with smiles and waves.

"Loco," he muttered. "Everybody down here is plumb loco."

30

In his lifetime Cherokee Joe Bunker had done his drinking in some ramshackle, rundown, rat-ridden saloons. He had tipped a bottle in places that would make a man sick in the daylight. He'd had to kick rats out of the way to get to the bar. Stacked up against some of these, the cantina in Los Perros was not so bad.

The bar, such as it was, consisted of a plank supported by four upended wooden barrels. There were half a dozen splintery tables with mismatched chairs. The place smelled of peppers and Mexicans.

Joe stopped inside the doorway to let his eyes get used to the dimness. The men standing at the make-shift bar and scattered among the tables watched him with hooded eyes.

He heard somebody whisper, "*El Furioso.*"

What the hell, Joe thought, it never hurt a man to have a rough-sounding handle.

He eased into a chair at an empty table and slapped the wooden tabletop with the flat of his hand.

"How about some service here?"

After a minute a thin Mexican with a pockmarked face came out from behind the bar. He sauntered over to Joe's table and stood with his arms folded.

"Whiskey," Joe said.

The Mexican continued to stare at him with no change in his expression.

"Whiskey," Joe said again, speaking louder. "You got any whiskey in this rat hole?"

The thin Mexican looked around the dim cantina at the other men, who were all watching him now. Nobody said anything. He turned back to Joe with a shrug.

"Dammit, don't any of you bean-eaters understand English?" Joe carried a hand up to his mouth in a drinking gesture. "Whiskey. Likker. Red-eye. Fetch me somethin' to drink before I keel over."

Slow understanding came into the eyes of the Mexican. "*Ah, licor!*"

"Now you got it, boy."

"*Pulque!*" the man said triumphantly. He turned to the others and repeated it. "*Pulque!*"

"*Pulque!*" they echoed cheerfully. "*Pulque por El Furioso!*"

"Whatever it is, bring me some," Joe said. Then, remembering one of his small store of Spanish words, "And hurry it up. *Pronto.*"

"*Pulque pronto,*" said the cantinero, amid much laughter from his customers. "*Pulque pronto. Sí.*"

He went back behind the plank bar and dipped something out of a clay crock into a huge cup. The other customers were grinning at Joe, showing signs of wanting to be friendly. Joe ignored them. When he chose drinking companions it would not be a bunch of raggedy peons who couldn't even talk his language.

The cantinero came back with the cup that held

close to a pint of murky liquid. He placed it on the table in front of Joe with a flourish. *"Pulque, senor."*

The stuff looked as appetizing as swamp water, and it smelled worse. But what the hell, Joe decided, this was probably as close as he would get to honest whiskey. He raised the cup and took a good swig. The temperature and the taste was about what he would expect from buffalo piss. He saw that everybody in the cantina was watching him, so he fought off the impulse to gag and swallowed the stuff. His stomach contracted at the shock, lurched dangerously, then started to grow warm. The warmth quickly spread throughout his body, all the way to his toes and the tips of his fingers.

"Not bad," he rasped to the hovering cantinero.

The other customers let go a cheer. Joe found himself grinning back at them. They raised their drinks in his direction. He hoisted his cup of buffalo piss back toward them, and everybody drank. He decided these people weren't a whole lot different from folks he'd met in saloons up north, even if they didn't know how to talk English. Joe took another swallow of the tepid liquor and decided it didn't taste all that bad either. Maybe the time he had to spend down here wouldn't be a total loss.

Two hours later Joe sat at a table in the center of the room surrounded by Mexicans. He had an arm around the man on either side of him, and was bellowing *The Yellow Rose of Texas* in a badly off-key baritone while his companions joined in with a marching song of Santa Anna's army. The cantinero kept the pulque flowing.

After the third repeat of the one chorus he knew, Joe felt somebody shaking his shoulder. He turned to stare into the face of the cantinero.

"What is it, *amigo*?" Joe said, brimming with good-fellowship.

The man answered with a burst of Spanish, of which Joe recognized only one word—*muchachas*. By following the man's vigorous pantomime, Joe finally got the message that there were some girls outside asking to see *El Furioso*.

Joe got to his feet, knocking the chair over backward. This brought whoops of laughter from the Mexicans. Joe laughed right along with them.

He walked across the room to the doorway, wondering why he hadn't noticed when he came in how uneven the floor was.

Outside the sunlight was harsh and bright. Joe blinked at the three girls who stood in the road waiting for him.

"Here I am," he announced, swaying slightly. "What's on your minds?"

The girls put hands over their mouths to stifle giggles. They looked about fifteen or sixteen. Joe thought he recognized them from the Gonzales family, but all Mexicans looked pretty much alike to him.

Two of the girls urged the other one forward. She cleared her throat. Speaking very deliberately, she announced, "*Señora* say you 'ave bat now." When she finished the speech she looked around at her friends for their approval.

Joe rubbed the back of his neck, trying to make sense out of the girl's words. "Bat? I don't have no bat. What in blazes are you talkin' about?"

The Mexican girl started over. "*Señora* say you 'ave bat now."

Joe wrinkled his brow and tried to figure it out. The pulque had dulled his thinking somewhat, but he would give it a try. The *señora* must be Jessie. She had sent the Gonzales girls down here to tell him something. Tell him he had a bat? No, that didn't make any sense. That Jessie had a bat and was waiting for him? Not likely. His brow creased in thought. The last time he had talked to Jessie she was getting ready to take her bath.

Bath.

Joe jabbed a grimy finger at the girl who had delivered the message. He fixed her with a ferocious glare.

"You can just go back and tell the *señora* that Cherokee Joe Bunker takes a bath only when and if he decides to. And if he decides not to take one at all, then he don't. You got that?"

The girl stared at the threatening finger, then smiled hopefully up at him.

"*Señora* say you 'ave bat now."

"Aw, the hell with it," Joe grumbled. "I'll tell her myself."

He started up the street toward Jessie's house. The Gonzales girls fell in step with him. One took each of his hands while the third danced along ahead. Joe started to pull free, but stopped when he realized he was kind of enjoying it. Besides the girls were having fun, so he relaxed and allowed them to lead him. Behind him, the men from the cantina were all standing out on the road laughing and calling out comments in Spanish that made the three girls blush and giggle.

They reached the end of the road and Joe started up the path to the house. The girls tugged him to a stop.

"What's the idea? I thought the *señora* wanted to see me."

"You 'ave bat now."

"Girl, I wish you'd learn some new words."

"Bat *now*," she insisted.

With two of them pulling him by the hands and the third pushing from behind, the Gonzales girls steered Joe toward the big iron cauldron. The remains of a wood fire still smoldered around the base.

"Hey!" Joe protested.

"Bat now."

"Just a blame minute. Are you tryin' to tell me that you girls are goin' to give me a bath?"

From the giggling and sidelong looks that passed among the girls, Joe figured they must have caught his meaning.

"Oh, no you ain't," he said firmly. "No twitterin' little chili-bean muchachas are gonna give no bath to Cherokee Joe Bunker."

The Gonzales girls merely continued to giggle and tug him toward the steaming cauldron. He could easily have pulled free of their grasp, but suddenly he found he did not really want to. Hell, there were harder things to take than being given a bath by three young girls who, when he stopped to think about it, weren't half bad looking, for Mexicans.

He allowed them to lead him up to the cauldron. There the girls started plucking at his buttons.

"Hold it!" he yelled. "This is somethin' I can durn well do for myself."

First he unhitched his gunbelt and lay it carefully on the ground within reach. Then he took off his coat, his shirt, his bandana, and his pants. He sat down and allowed the girls to pull off his boots and wool socks. He stood up then and started to step up on the box that had been placed next to the cauldron. The girls began chattering in Spanish and pulling at his union suit.

"Oh, no you don't. I ain't takin' that off with no females around," he announced. "Why, I'd be buck nekkid."

The girls giggled, but continued to hold onto his union suit.

"Aw what the hell," he said, "if you ain't seen it before, you won't know what it is." He shucked out of the underwear and stepped into the steaming water. He let out a yell.

"What are you tryin' to do, cook me alive?" Slowly he eased down to a squatting position that brought the waterline up to his neck. As a last hold on dignity, he kept his greasy sombrero firmly planted on his head.

The Gonzales girls produced a brick of harsh yellow soap and three scrub brushes with bristles like barbed wire. They attacked the bathing of Joe Bunker with wild enthusiasm. Ignoring his yells and protests, they scrubbed every inch of his hide until he glowed like a baby and the water in the cauldron was black. In the end he even let them take off his hat and scrub his scalp until it felt like he'd lost an argument to an Indian.

When he was finally clean enough to satisfy the Gonzaleses, they made him get out of the cauldron and stand while they poured cold, clean rinse water over him. He toweled himself dry, feeling better than he thought was possible. The glow from the pulque had been cooked out of him, but he had a healthy, hungry feel that took ten years off his age.

The girls gave him a shirt of soft white cotton and a pair of clean pants to put on. They gave him to understand that his own duds would be laundered, or burned, he couldn't make out which they meant. It didn't really matter. What he wanted right that minute was to be with Jessie McKee.

He picked up his gunbelt and started toward the house. The girls stood back watching him, whispering and giggling among themselves. Joe turned to give them one of his darkest scowls. It only made them laugh all the more. Joe gave up and grinned back at them. There was no use trying to fool somebody who's just given you a bath.

He walked into the house and looked around. At first he thought no one was there, then he saw Jessie in the bed. It was all made up with fresh linen sheets she had got from God-knew-where. There were a pair of plump pillows up at the head, and Jessie's hair spilled across them like liquid copper.

"Hello, Jessie."

"Hello, Joe. I see you got your bath."

"I think them muchachas of yours took off half my hide."

"Are you going to hang up those guns and come to bed, or are you going to stand there staring at me?"

"Truth to tell, Jessie, you look so damn purty, I almost hate to muss you up."

"Get over here and muss me up, you curly wolf, before I come out and get you."

Joe took off the clean Mexican clothes and got into bed beside Jessie. He folded back the sheet that covered her and ran his eyes over her long, firm body.

"You know, Jessie," he said, "as many times as we've rolled in the hay together, I ain't never really took the time for a good look at you."

"Now that you're looking, do you like what you see?"

"You are one hell of a beautiful woman, Redhead."

Jessie started to reply, but never got the words out. Suddenly there were tears in her eyes.

"What's the matter?" Joe said. "What are you cryin' for?"

"I'm crying because I'm happy, you damn fool. Don't you know anything about women?"

"Precious little," Joe admitted.

She held out her arms to him, and he took her and held her, and it was as though it was happening for the first time for both of them. There was no need now for the game of roughhouse they had always played in bed. Their feelings for each other came out now in gentle touches and whispered words, and in urgent longings and joyful cries. It was a long, long night.

31

THE next two days were different for Cherokee Joe Bunker than anything he had known in his forty years. He was actually happy. He walked around with a foolish grin on his face, feeling uncommonly good about everything.

In his eyes the grubby town of Los Perros had become an enchanted village. Its people were the friendliest, best-looking, warmest folks he had ever met. The one-room adobe house he shared with Jessie was their palace. Although he would have bitten through his tongue before saying it aloud, Cherokee Joe was in love.

When he was married to the mother of his boys Joe was a young man full of piss and vinegar who didn't feel a whole lot of affection for anybody. Elvira was a girl of simple tastes, content to wait patiently for Joe to come to her. What with carousing with the boys and robbing stagecoaches, Joe was away from home a lot more than he was there. Still, he felt bad when Elvira died in the winter of 1842. Not a lot worse than when his favorite horse succumbed to the colic, but he did miss her.

There had been other women after Elvira's passing. Plenty of them. But they came and went so fast Joe hardly ever got to know their names. Living the kind of life he did, on the run much of the time, he felt he could not afford to get attached to any woman.

Then he met Jessie McKee and everything changed. Here was a woman who was not intimidated by his scowl, and who yelled right back at him when he hollered.

Right from the first there was a contest between them over who was going to be the boss. They worked it out by deciding that Jessie would tell him what to do in the daytime, when she was paying his salary, but when the lights went out at night it was Joe's turn.

Until Los Perros the arrangement had worked out nicely. Both Joe and Jessie got their needs taken care of, and neither of them got tied down with any promises or vows of affection. But after their first night together in the Mexican village everything was different.

Neither of them put it into words the next day, but they both felt the change. Little smiles were passed back and forth. They found excuses to touch each other. Jessie forgot about treating him like an employee in the daytime, and Joe was relieved that he did not have to dominate her any more in bed.

Joe was surprised to discover that Jessie was good to talk to, even when they weren't in bed. He always figured women were for breeding and housekeeping, and if a man wanted to talk serious he went and found him another man. They spent the two days entirely in each other's company like two people getting to know each other. Which they were.

On their third evening in Los Perros, Joe and Jessie

sat together on the wooden step outside the adobe house. Joe wore his white Mexican clothes, and Jessie had on a figured skirt and deep-cut blouse lent her by one of the Gonzales girls. Inside the house Mamacita Gonzales was cooking up something spicy. Nearby two small boys played with a black-and-brown puppy. From the cantina they could hear guitar music and a man's voice singing a mournful love song.

Jessie rubbed her cheek against his shoulder. "Do you want to hear something crazy, Joe?"

"Sure."

"I almost wish Smiler would never show up with the greenbacks."

"That *is* crazy," Joe agreed. "Them greenbacks are the whole reason we're down here."

"Yes, I know. But these last couple of days have been so peaceful. All my life I've been fighting with somebody. Always working my tail off to prove I can do something as good as a man. Here I don't have to fight with anybody and I don't have to prove anything. I wish it could just go on this way."

For a long time Joe didn't say anything. Finally he cleared his throat. "Jessie, I been thinkin'."

"About what?"

"About when we leave here, what we're gonna do. Once Smiler and Jack get here, and we divide up the money you get for the greenbacks, what happens to us?"

"What do you mean, Joe?"

"I mean, dammit, that you and me can't just go back to the way things was before. It's different between us now."

"Yes, it is different." Jessie's voice was gentle.

"Even if we wanted to, we couldn't pick up where we left off, since there ain't no more Ace Freighters."

Jessie waited for him to go on.

"What I'm tryin' to tell you, woman, is that I don't want to ride on alone after this. I want you with me." Joe glanced over his shoulder as though to see who had spoken. Mamacita was still inside the house, and none of the other Gonzaleses were within earshot. "Dammit, Jessie," he blurted, "I'll even marry you, if that's what it takes."

Jessie leaned back and looked at him. Joe stared self-consciously out over the desert.

"You don't have to do that, Joe," she said. "We can still be together without getting married. We have this long."

Joe sighed heavily. "You sure do make it tough for a man. I'm sayin' I *want* to marry you. I want to walk into a room full of people with you on my arm and say to everybody straight out, this here's my wife."

"Are you sure that's what you want, Joe? It's not just because we're alone down here and there's a big moon at night? This is the first time, you know, that we've really been by ourselves, without a lot of other people around."

"Not counting Gonzaleses," Joe said.

Jessie laughed with him. "That's right, not counting Gonzaleses."

He grew serious. " 'Course, I ain't no prize as a husband, but I reckon I can straighten up somewhat. I'll take a bath every week if you want. Hell, twice a week. I ain't sayin' I'll turn into no saint, but I'll treat you as good as I know how, Jessie."

She took his big callused hand in hers and pressed it to her cheek. "Don't go making a whole lot of rash promises now."

"Don't worry, I don't aim to promise nothin' I can't deliver."

"Then I say let's do it, Joe. Let's get married. And I promise you that I'll be one hell of a wife."

Joe broke into a wide grin. "I know that, Redhead. Oh, my, I do know that."

Mamacita Gonzales loomed in the doorway behind them and beamed down at the lovers.

Joe turned and tried unsuccessfully to scowl at her. "What are you grinnin' at?"

"You eat now," said the round Mexican woman.

"I see you been givin' her English lessons," Joe said to Jessie.

"*Pronto*," Mamacita added, and disappeared back into the house.

"These people get right bossy if you let 'em," Joe said.

"We'd better go in," Jessie said, laughing. "Mamacita is used to running things around here."

As they stood up, Jessie stopped and clapped her hands like a little girl. "Oh, look at those lovely flowers over by the cactus. The red ones and the yellow. Wouldn't they look nice on our table?"

"I guess so, if a person likes flowers," Joe said. "I'll go get 'em for you."

"No, you go inside," Jessie told him. "Picking flowers is the woman's job. I'll just be a minute."

She squeezed Joe's hand, and he went on into the house. The clump of cactus was about twenty yards away. As Jessie crossed the hard packed ground she saw the black and brown puppy dashing in excited circles. When he saw her approaching, the little dog bounded over.

"What's the matter," she said, "did your little friends go away and leave you all alone?"

The puppy braced its stubby legs and barked at her. The little tail wagged itself into a blur.

"Sorry, I haven't time to play with you now." Jessie smiled at herself. "Here I am talking to a dog. And in English to a Mexican dog. I must really be in love."

Smiling at her foolishness, Jessie picked up her skirt to step across the prickly pear to the taller cactus where the flowers grew. She heard the angry buzzing sound and stopped. She froze for an instant at the sight of the big diamondback coiled among the cactus. In that instant it struck her.

The rattler hit her high on the fleshy part of the thigh, above the top of her stocking. The curved fangs pierced the skin and sank into the muscle tissue.

Jessie stood in shock, staring down at the writhing snake that was still clamped to her leg. The tail lashed about, the rattle buzzing. At last she caught her breath and screamed.

Inside the house Joe was just settling into his chair at the dinner table when he heard Jessie's cry. Instantly he was on his feet running out the door, the Walker Colt cocked in his right hand.

He saw Jessie dancing around crazily by the cactus patch. She screamed again and struck at the snake, which still clung obscenely to her upper leg.

As Joe pounded up Jessie finally managed to knock the rattler away from her. It hit the ground with a fat *plop* and slithered toward the shelter of the cactus.

Joe took in the situation with a glance, leveled his revolver, and fired. The snake's head disappeared in a spray of pink. Joe fanned off three more shots, each smashing into the still-writhing body of the snake. He cursed mindlessly.

When at last he turned from the remains of the diamondback, he found Jessie holding her skirt up, rubbing the inside of her thigh.

"The bastard got me, Joe," she said.

"Let's have a look." He helped her sit down and tucked the skirt up around her waist. While several Gonzaleses approached cautiously, Joe bent down to examine the two little puncture wounds in Jessie's silky skin. The area around them was already turning dark.

Joe swore between his clenched teeth. He looked up at the circle of brown faces.

"Have you got a doctor?"

They looked at him blankly.

"A doctor, Goddamnit! We need a doctor."

The Mexicans looked at each other and back at Joe. Their liquid brown eyes were sympathetic, but puzzled.

"What's the fuckin' Mex word for fuckin' doctor?" Joe growled.

"It's *médico*," Jessie said. Her voice was thin and unnatural.

"*Médico!*" he shouted at the villagers. "Get me a Goddamned *médico*, you stupid fuckin' bean-eaters!"

One of them spoke to him in soft, rapid Spanish. Joe did not understand the words, but his heart sank as he caught the negative tone in the man's voice.

"It's no good, Joe," Jessie said. "There's no doctor within a day's ride."

"Jumping Christ! What the hell do these people do when they get sick?"

"They get better by themselves," Jessie said. "Or they die."

"Well, by God, you ain't gonna die if I got anything to say about it." Joe scooped her into his arms and started toward the house. Jessie was not a small woman, but he carried her as though she were a child. The Mexican villagers parted quickly to make way for him. Several of the Gonzaleses followed him inside.

He lay Jessie down on the bed. Her face was flushed, and there was a sheen of perspiration on her

forehead. Joe removed the shoe and stocking from the
injured leg. The discolored patch of skin around the
puncture was larger now. Dark little shoots grew out of
it like the claws of a crab.

"Mamacita!" Joe called.

The Mexican woman hurried to his side. "*Señor?*"

Joe drew the Bowie knife from his belt. Using pantomime to illustrate his words he said, "Put this blade
in the fire. Make it hot. *Mucho* hot. Understand? *Com-
prende?*"

"*Sí.*" She took the knife from Joe and hurried across
to the hearth. There she held it with the blade down
where the coals glowed red-orange.

At bedside, Joe pulled the bandana from his neck. A
clean one, for a change, thanks to the laundering of the
Gonzales girls. He dipped it into the bucket of cool
drinking water, wrung it out, and used it to mop Jessie's
face.

"I don't feel so good, Joe," she said.

"I know, Redhead. You rest easy as you can and I'll
see what I can do to make you feel better."

"You were right, Joe," she said weakly.

"What say?"

"You were right. I shouldn't have stopped you from
shooting that rattler the other day when you wanted
to."

"Hell, this prob'ly wasn't even the same critter."

"From now on you make all the decisions. I won't
ever go against you again."

" 'Course you will," Joe said. "What fun would it be
havin' a woman around who never argued? You hush
now and let me work on this little nip."

Mamacita brought the knife back to Joe. He could
feel the heat of the blade when he held it near his arm.

He wrung out the bandana again and handed it to Jessie.

"You might want to chew on that whilst I make a little nick in your leg here."

Jessie looked at him with huge frightened eyes. She twisted the bandana into a rope and clamped it between her teeth.

"That's the girl. You just think about somethin' real nice now. Somethin' purty and soft."

He leaned down close to the puncture wounds. Mamacita brought a lamp and held it to throw the most light on Jessie's leg. Joe drew a deep breath and sliced into her flesh. Jessie grunted. He looked up at her and she shook her head to indicate she was all right.

Joe worked swiftly and made a little "X" cut a quarter of an inch deep over each of the punctures. Dark, angry blood welled up and trickled down her thigh. Joe laid the knife aside. He put his mouth over the wound and sucked.

Mixed with the salt of Jessie's blood he could taste the bitter snake venom. One of the Gonzales children came running with a basin. He spat the black, tainted blood into it and returned to the wound. Again and again he sucked the wound and spat into the basin, until the blood was pinkish red and he could no longer taste the poison. The flesh was pale white around the punctures now, but there was an evil dark halo farther out. Joe winced as he saw the dark streaks crawling up Jessie's leg to her crotch.

He covered her up and laid a hand on her forehead. The fever was rising.

"Did you get it all, Joe?" she asked.

"As much as I could. Did it hurt?"

She gave him a weak smile. "It felt kind of good.

When I'm feeling better we'll have to do some experimenting."

Her body began to shake. "It gets cold fast down here at night."

"I'll have Mamacita build up the fire." He took his mackinaw from a peg on the wall and laid it gently atop the blanket that covered her.

"Joe?"

"Yeah?"

"Is it bad?"

"Hell, it's just a little snakebite. I've knowed lots of men bit worse'n that scarcely felt it. Shoot, by mornin' you'll be prancin' around here as ornery as ever."

"You wouldn't lie to me, would you?"

"Only if I could get away with it."

"Well, you can't, so you better not try."

"I'll keep that in mind," he said.

The night was the longest in Cherokee Joe's memory. Jessie's fever continued to climb, although she lay shivering in the bed as though she were packed in ice. Joe climbed into bed with her and held her against his body. That seemed to help with the chills, but she began drifting in and out of delirium. She talked of people and places that had no meaning for Joe. She vomited until he could swear her stomach held nothing more, then she vomited again. During the periods when she was lucid she clung tightly to Joe's neck and begged for reassurance that she was going to be all right. He told her she was, but he knew it was a lie.

Mamacita and the older Gonzales children took turns keeping the fire going and bringing fresh cool cloths for Jessie's head. They were so honestly concerned that Joe wished he had the words to thank them properly.

Several times during the night he fell into a light doze, only to be jolted awake by Jessie's delirious shouts, or when her body shook with a new chill. He began to think the morning would never come.

But the morning did come. The sky was high and blue with a gentle breeze blowing in from the west. The flowers Jessie had admired were an explosion of color against the brown landscape. The day was beautiful, but within Joe Bunker's heart it was the darkest day of the world.

Jessie looked bad. Her upper leg and groin were swollen and discolored. Pus oozed from the crosscuts made by Joe's knife. Her face was drawn, her eyes glassy with fever.

"I'm goin' to ride for a doctor," Joe told her. "I don't know what more to do for you."

She reached out from the bed and seized his hand with surprising strength.

"Don't leave me, Joe. There's no time for you to find a doctor. I'm afraid to be alone. Promise you won't leave me. Promise."

Joe brought his other hand over to clasp Jessie's between both of his. He was shocked at how fragile the bones felt. "I won't leave you, Redhead. I promise."

Mamacita brought a bowl of clear broth, but Jessie turned her head away, unable even to taste it. Joe waved away the burrito Mamacito had prepared for him. He continued to sit by the bed holding Jessie's hand.

By the middle of the morning her breathing was very shallow. Her heartbeat was faint and fluttery. Joe kept the blanket over her swollen leg so Jessie would not see how bad it looked.

He sent one of the young Gonzales boys to the cantina for a flask of pulque. If Jessie could keep it down, he figured it might ease her pain somewhat. And a couple of good swallows wouldn't do him any harm either.

After a minute the Gonzales boy came running back empty handed.

"Where's the pulque?" Joe said.

The boy pointed excitedly out the door toward the town. *"Gringo! Gringo!"*

"What are you talkin' about, boy? What gringo?"

A tall narrow shadow filled the doorway.

"Howdy," said Smiler. "Anybody here want a million dollars?"

32

CHEROKEE Joe stared up at Smiler from where he knelt beside Jessie's bed. He did not speak.

"Is this any way to greet a man who's just spent two weeks in the saddle?" Smiler came into the room and stopped at the foot of the bed. He looked down at Jessie. "What's the matter with her?"

"Snake bit her," Joe said.

"Well, ain't that one hell of a note. How bad is she?"

Joe placed a hand on Jessie's forehead. The skin was hot and dry to his touch. "Bad," he said.

Smiler glared at the Mexicans who were standing at a respectful distance. "Can't these greasers do anything for her?"

"They ain't doctors," Joe said. "There ain't a doctor in the whole territory."

Smiler dropped a pair of heavy saddlebags to the floor. "What are we supposed to do if she dies?"

Joe stared at him coldly. "I think we're supposed to bury her."

"I mean, what are we supposed to do with these

244

here greenbacks? I took a lot of chances to get 'em and bring 'em down here. Jessie said she knew how to change 'em for real money, but we're out of luck if she croaks."

"Smiler, you're commencin' to aggravate me."

"Now don't get all riled up, Joe. All I'm sayin' is that we'll be in a hell of a fix tryin' to get rid of this paper without Jessie, and we ought to be thinkin' about it."

Jessie stirred on the bed. Joe turned away from Smiler to look at her.

"The house is burning," she said. "Get everybody out. Where's Beth? Has anybody seen my little girl?"

"What's she talkin' about?" Smiler said.

"It's the fever," Joe told him.

"We've got to get out of here," Jessie said. "The fire!"

"She's plumb loco," Smiler said.

Joe stared at him thoughtfully. "Where's Jack?"

Smiler put on a mournful face. "I'm sorry, Joe, but I got some bad news for you."

Joe stood up. "What's happened to my boy?"

"We ran into some trouble at White Horse Springs."

Joe turned to the Mexican woman who was standing quietly across the room. "Mamacita."

"*Sí?*"

Joe nodded down at Jessie, who was dozing fitfully again. "You watch the *senora*."

The woman nodded her understanding and came over to sit beside the bed.

Joe walked out through the doorway and beckoned to Smiler to follow. They stopped a short distance from the house and faced each other.

"I want you tell me about the trouble at White Horse Springs," Joe said.

"There wasn't nothin' I could do, Joe. One of them people at the station had a gambler's gun hid in his boot. Whilst I was marchin' the other one out back, he pulled the hideaway pistol and shot Jack."

"Kill him?"

"He died in my arms."

Joe squinted off toward the horizon. "That's peculiar. It ain't like one of my boys to get fooled by a boot gun."

"It was the kid's first job," Smiler said. "I reckon he was a mite jumpy."

"You coulda looked out for him."

"I did everything a man could, Joe. Like I told you, I was off in back of the station when he got shot."

"Damn," Joe said to the empty desert. "Damn, damn, damn."

"The varmint won't sneak-shoot another man," Smiler said. "I gunned him down. His partner too."

"That don't help my boy none," Joe said.

Mamacita appeared suddenly in the doorway. *"Sénor! Adelante!"*

Joe took off running for the house. Smiler followed more slowly. Mamacita stepped aside as Joe rushed in. Jessie was sitting up in bed. For a moment Joe's heart leaped, thinking she had passed the crisis. Then he drew near and saw the unnatural fever brightness of her eyes."

"Joe?" her voice was like the rustle of dry leaves.

"I'm here, Jessie."

"I'm feeling a whole lot better."

"Good. That's real good. You oughtn't to tire yourself by sittin' up like that, though. Why don't you just lay back down there."

Joe eased her head back down onto the pillow. He spread the rich auburn hair about her face.

She looked up at him with glittering intensity. "What you said about us getting married. Did you mean it?"

"I meant it," Joe said.

She smiled weakly. Her eyes seemed to lose their focus. "I'm glad. I'm tired of being alone, Joe. I'm real tired."

"You won't be alone no more, Redhead. I promise you that."

"What kind of a house will we live in, Joe?"

"What kind do you want?"

"A big house."

"We'll build one as big as you want."

"Then my Beth can come and visit us. Your boys, too."

"Sure, Jessie."

Her smile switched off. She reached out with both hands and grasped Joe's shirt. With a strength that surprised him she pulled him down close to her.

"I'm dying, Joe."

"No, you ain't. Don't you even think that. You're gonna get better. You'll see."

"No. I'm dying, and I'm afraid. I want you to hold me."

Joe put his arms around her. He was shocked at how thin she felt. Jessie clung to him, her breath shallow and rapid in his ear. Her body jerked convulsively. There was a terrible deep rattle in her throat. The fingers gripping his shirt gradually relaxed.

Very gently Joe placed Jessie's arms down at her sides. With the ball of his thumb he closed her eyelids.

"Is she dead?" Smiler said.

Still sitting on the bed, Joe turned to look at Smiler in the doorway.

"She's dead."

Mamacita began to cry softly.

"Damn her eyes," Smiler said.

"What was that?"

"Look, Joe, I know you and Jessie had a thing goin' together, but that don't count for nothin' now. That bitch talked us all into goin' along with this fool idea, and now you and me are stuck in this greaser town with a million dollars we can't spend and a heap of trouble waitin' for us north of the border."

Cherokee Joe stood up slowly and faced him. "Let's go outside, Smiler."

After a moment, Smiler backed slowly out the door. Joe took his gunbelt from the wall peg, buckled it on, then followed.

When they were away from the house Joe said, "I don't like you, Smiler. I never did have any use for you. And I ain't goin' to listen to you cuss out a woman I thought very highly of."

"Simmer down, Joe. I didn't mean to be disrespectful to Jessie."

"Like hell you didn't." Joe waited. When there was no response, he went on. "Somethin' else is botherin' me, Smiler. I flat don't believe your story about what happened to my boy Jack."

"Are you sayin' I didn't tell it true?"

"More than that. I'm sayin' you're a yellow-livered, scum-suckin' mangy dog of a liar."

Smiler's face paled. His malformed lip twitched, but he said nothing.

In the street below them, the men of the Mexican village stood silently watching the two gringos face off. The sun beat down mercilessly.

"I'm givin' you a chance to go for your gun, Smiler," Joe said. "You got a count of ten to draw first. If your hand's still empty when I finish countin', I'll kill you anyhow."

Smiler sucked in a breath. The air hissed through his exposed teeth.

"One," Joe began. "Two . . . Three . . ."

"Señor! Señor!"

The two men turned to see one of the young Gonzales boys running toward them down the hill that rose behind Jessie's house.

"Gringo!" the boy cried, pointing behind him. *"Un otro gringo!"*

"There's another white man comin'," Joe said. "Was you followed down here?"

"No," said Smiler. "I kept watch all the way, and nobody got on my trail."

"Well, somebody's found us. You and me can settle our quarrel later. Right now we better get set where we can see this stranger before he sees us."

Smiler nodded grimly. He took a rifle from his saddle and climbed up on the roof of the adobe at the head of the dusty street. Joe positioned himself on the roof across from him. From there they would have a good shot at the approaching rider. Below them, the street was suddenly empty.

33

CHEROKEE Joe crouched behind the low parapet that bordered the roof of the adobe. He shaded his eyes and squinted across the dazzling sand toward the hill where the rider would come in. It seemed unlikely that a lone lawman would have followed Smiler, but it was foolish to take chances. Joe had done all the time in prison he ever intended to do.

Across the way sunlight glinted off the barrel of Smiler's rifle. Funny, Joe thought, how a minute ago they were ready to kill each other, and now they were on the same side. But it was only temporary. There was no way, Joe knew, that the both of them would walk out of Los Perros alive.

The head and shoulders of the lone rider appeared above the rise behind Jessie's house. Joe steadied the heavy Walker Colt on the edge of the parapet and thumbed the hammer back. He did not want to bushwhack anybody, but if there was a posse following the stranger, Joe intended to go down fighting.

The rider crested the hill and started slowly down the sandy slope toward the village. The short hairs prickled on the back of Joe's neck. There was something achingly familiar about the way the rider sat his horse. The erect posture, the careless way he gripped the reins. Morgan!

Joe stood up waving his arms. At the same instant he saw Smiler raise the rifle.

"Dive, Morgan!"

It was a game the three of them had played when the boys were little. Joe would hide behind a bush or something while Jack and Morgan raced around looking for him. Suddenly he would jump out and shout, "Dive!" The boys would hit the dirt rolling around and laughing while he roughhoused with them.

He heard the crack of Smiler's rifle and saw Morgan spill from the saddle. Then he was looking across the road into the rifle barrel as Smiler fired again.

Morgan was startled when he saw the man suddenly stand up on the roof of the adobe, then when he heard the cry from out of his childhood, instinct took over. He threw himself from the saddle as the rifle cracked, and rolled over and over in the dirt.

Another rifle shot. Morgan looked up to see the standing man frozen for an instant, and he knew it was his father. The pistol fell from Cherokee Joe's hand, and he somersaulted forward off the roof. He landed hard on his back in the street below, raising a puff of dust, and lay still.

Morgan went into a crouching, zig-zagging run toward the cover offered by the house directly below him. There were no more shots fired. The momentary distraction by Cherokee Joe had saved his life.

He leaned against the back wall of the house while his breathing quieted, and studied his situation. He had not got a good look at the rifleman, but it couldn't be anybody but Smiler Tate. The rifle gave Smiler an advantage at long range, so Morgan had to somehow get close enough for his Navy Colts to even up the fight.

He poked his head around the corner of the building for a fraction of a second and pulled it back as the rifle barked and the bullet bit out a chunk of adobe.

Morgan squinted up at the sun and reckoned it was just past noon. He did not dare venture into the open in the daylight, so his best bet was to hole up somewhere until nightfall.

The house he was using for cover had no back door. There was just a small window with a woven curtain hanging on the inside. Morgan slid along the wall to the window, pushed the curtain aside, and looked in. It was dim inside, but he could make out a figure lying on the bed and a stout Mexican woman standing by the hearth, watching him. Morgan showed the woman his gun and put a finger to his lips. She nodded to show she understood.

He levered himself up onto the window ledge and squirmed through headfirst onto the floor. The Mexican woman pressed back against the far wall.

"Don't be afraid," Morgan told her. "I won't hurt you." He searched his memory for the Spanish words. "*No molesto*," he said, pointing the gun up in the air.

The woman seemed reassured, but she continued to watch him warily.

Morgan wondered why the person lying on the bed did not move at all the commotion. He got to his feet and edged over that way. Then he saw the red hair spread over the pillow, and went closer.

Jessie McKee was drawn and pale. There were discolored patches under eyes, and the bones showed through her hands. Still, there was a peacefulness in her face that Morgan had never seen while she lived.

Remembering an afternoon in a Sacramento Hotel, Morgan drew the blanket up gently to cover her face.

He moved to the wall next to the doorway. From there he could keep an eye on the corner of the roof where Smiler had concealed himself. All that was visible now was the end of the rifle barrel and the very tip of Smiler's hat. The spot where Cherokee Joe had fallen was beyond Morgan's field of vision.

He hated to leave his father lying out there exposed to the sun, but there was no way he could reach the body without presenting an open target for the rifle. His only objective now was to kill Smiler Tate. He would let nothing deter him.

The hours crawled by. To fill in the time while he waited for dark, Morgan poked through the contents of a pair of heavy saddlebags he found lying on the floor. He recognized the greenbacks immediately as the loot from the White Horse Springs robbery. He counted the bills up to $500,000, matched the pile against those had not yet counted, and calculated that the whole million dollars was there.

From time to time he peeked out the doorway, but never saw more of Smiler than the gun barrel and the tip of his hat. He wondered where the villagers were. Aside from the stout woman who sat quietly across the room from him, he had seen no one. He chewed on a cold tortilla he found on the table, and hoped Smiler was getting good and hungry.

At long last the sun slipped below the horizon. In the twilight shadows Morgan saw dark shapes moving in the desert. The people of the village. They showed no eagerness to return until the foreigners had finished their bloody business.

When he felt it was dark enough, Morgan drew in a deep breath and dashed through the doorway out of his shelter. He sprinted across the hard ground to the building where Smiler was. There he fetched up against the wall. The adobe retained a residue of warmth from the vanished sun.

He held his breath, listening. The only sounds were the rustlings of small desert animals in the night. A half-moon gave just enough light for Morgan to locate the corner of the building where the adobe bricks projected from the wall enough to leave cracks for hand and footholds.

He started up the wall. It was an awkward business climbing with the pistol in his right hand, but when he reached the roof Morgan wanted to be ready to shoot.

A step at a time he crawled upward, alert for any sound from above. At last he reached the parapet and raised his head for a look. There in the far corner was the huddled figure with the end of the rifle barrel and the tip of the hat extending above the wall. Morgan took aim.

"Smiler!"

The figure did not move. Instead, a pistol barked somewhere on the ground behind him. The bullet chipped the wall an inch from Morgan's nose and sang off into the night.

Morgan let go the bricks and dropped to the hard-packed ground. His ankle bent painfully inward as he landed, but he could worry about that later. The important thing now was to keep moving and hold onto his gun.

He ran to the next building, gritting his teeth against the pain that shot up his leg. He crouched low against the wall and listened. Somewhere in the night another set of running footsteps echoed his own. They stopped a second later, and there was silence.

Morgan moved more slowly, making as little noise

as possible. At each building he stopped to listen. He heard nothing.

As he came to the last building on the street, there was a sound inside. A muffled *clunk* of glass or pottery. Morgan crept closer to the open doorway. Something padded across the floor inside.

The partial moon was on the far side of the building so Morgan would not be silhouetted as he entered. Still, he took the precaution of dropping to his hands and knees, well below the height where a waiting gunman would aim. Slowly, silently, he crawled into the dark interior.

Morgan's heart almost stopped when something cold and moist touched his face. He reached out instinctively and grasped the furry coat of a puppy. Just as he let out his breath in relief, a torch flared behind him.

"Stay right where you are, boy," said Smiler.

Shadows danced across the walls as Smiler carried the torch inside. Morgan saw by the tables and the rude bar that he was in a cantina. In his hands-and-knees position he had no chance to bring his gun into play. He turned his head to look up at Smiler.

"Well, well, the last of the Bunkers. The three of you have given me a passel of trouble, but it looks like I outlasted you."

"Not quite, you sonofabitch," rasped a voice from the doorway.

Smiler whirled to see Cherokee Joe standing there, his face set and pale like an avenging ghost. The front of his shirt was crimson.

The momentary distraction was enough. Morgan wheeled the Colt and fired. A pink spray of brains with slivers of skull blew out the far side of Smiler's head. His lifeless body flopped to the floor.

Morgan scrambled to retrieve the torch, then hurried

to his father's side. Cherokee Joe was leaning back against the wall next to the doorway. He slid slowly down to a sitting position.

"Pa, I thought you was dead when I saw you pitch off that roof," Morgan said.

Joe coughed painfully. "I might as well be, son. Smiler hit me a good one. I had just enough left to drag myself up here when I saw the torch." He coughed again. Bright red blood pumped out of the hole in his chest.

"Don't try to talk, Pa," Morgan said. "You'll tire yourself."

"It don't matter any more," said Joe. "I've used up my time. I want you to always——"

Joe never finished the sentence. His head flopped forward onto his chest, and Morgan knew it was over.

"Don't worry, Pa," he whispered. "I always will."

It was the middle of the morning on the following day when Morgan rode out of Los Perros. He paused on the crest of a hill to look back. The villagers once again went quietly about their business. On the slope behind the largest house were two graves side by side. At the far end of the street, all alone, was a third.

Morgan turned away for the last time. He adjusted the heavy saddlebags and clucked to his horse. He had a long way to ride, and somebody waiting.

THE END